BIG BIG
Story Book

WHITMAN PUBLISHING COMPANY
RACINE, WISCONSIN

CONTENTS

JASPER GIRAFFE
By Polly Ferrell

In the middle of Ungle Bungle Jungle stands Polly Parrot's Post Office. Every day all the animals who live in the jungle come to get their mail or to post the letters they have written.

Jasper Giraffe came running on his long legs every morning to see if he had any mail. But he never got any, and that always made him very sad.

One morning Jasper was feeling so sad that he didn't look where he was going. When you don't look where you are going, you sometimes fall down. And that is just what happened to Jasper. He fell down.

"Did you hurt yourself?" asked Polly Parrot.

"I think I have broken my leg," cried Jasper. "Nobody loves me," he sobbed. "I never get any letters." And he went limping away to his mamma.

A little later when Mrs. Elephant came to the post

5

office, Polly Parrot gave her a large, pink envelope and said, "Did you know that Jasper Giraffe fell down and broke his leg?"

"You don't say," said Mrs. Elephant.

"I just *did* say," said Polly Parrot.

"So you did," said Mrs. Elephant, and she went away carrying the big, pink envelope in her trunk.

Mrs. Elephant had just gone when Mrs. Monkey came into the post office with little Mabel and Minnie Monkey.

Mrs. Monkey got two letters and a big package.

Minnie Monkey told Polly Parrot she was learning to swing by her tail.

Then Polly Parrot said, "Did you know that Jasper Giraffe fell down and broke his leg?"

"You don't say!" said Mrs. Monkey.

"I just *did* say," said Polly Parrot.

"So you did," said Mrs. Monkey, and off she went with her babies.

In a little while Mrs. Kangaroo came hopping into the post office. Baby Kangaroo was peeking out of her pouch and smiling brightly.

Polly Parrot handed Mrs. Kangaroo a letter and a post card and said, "Did you know that Jasper Giraffe fell down and broke his leg?"

"You don't say!" said Mrs. Kangaroo.

"I just *did* say," said Polly Parrot.

"So you did," said Mrs. Kangaroo, as she put the mail into her pouch with Baby and started on her way home.

Just as Mrs. Kangaroo disappeared down the path, Miss Zebra came prancing up to the post office. She always pranced for she was always happy.

Polly Parrot looked through the letters and packages that were left and handed Miss Zebra a large blue envelope and a small package.

Then Polly Parrot said, "Did you know that Jasper Giraffe fell down and broke his leg?"

"You don't say!" said Miss Zebra.

"I just *did* say," said Polly Parrot.

"So you did," said Miss Zebra as she pranced off taking her mail with her.

All day long, as the animals came to get their mail or to post the letters they had written, Polly Parrot

told them about Jasper Giraffe. By the time the sun went down, every animal in the jungle had heard the news.

Next morning the post office was full of mail.

There were big letters, small letters, thick letters, and thin letters.

There were letters in green and pink and yellow envelopes. There were packages, too—big and little. And every single one was addressed to Jasper Giraffe.

Polly Parrot gathered up the letters and packages and took them to Jasper's house. Jasper was sitting on his front porch looking very sad. He had a bandage on one of his big, long legs.

"Hello, Polly Parrot," he said. "Somebody's getting a lot of letters. I wish I were. Where are you taking those letters and packages?"

"Every one is addressed to *Jasper Giraffe*," Polly Parrot answered, holding some up for him to read.

"You don't say," said Jasper.

"I just *did* say," Polly replied.

"So you did," said Jasper, and he glanced at all the addresses.

Then he *did* believe they were for him and he was so happy he laughed and laughed.

"You see," said Polly Parrot, "all the animals do love you and they are sorry you have a broken leg."

"But I do not have a broken leg," Jasper said, laughing. "I only scratched my knee."

"You don't say!" said Polly.

"I just *did* say," said Jasper.

"So you did," said Polly Parrot.

CHIPPER

Chipper was a lazy dog;
    He didn't like to run;
He didn't like to jump or bark
    Or play with anyone.

Every day he'd sit and watch
    The dogs across the street.
They ran and barked and jumped all day,
    And hardly stopped to eat.

"Those dogs are silly," Chipper said,
    "To wear themselves all out.
See how they wag and wag their tails
    Each time their masters shout."

So then he'd yawn and lie right down
    Beside his doghouse door,
And eat and sleep and dream of bones
    And wake and eat some more.

But Chipper didn't realize,
    While all day long he sat
And watched his neighbors exercise,
    That he was growing FAT.

Until one day a storm blew up.
    When it began to pour,
He stretched and slowly shook himself
    And started through his door.

But suddenly, to his surprise,
    The door began to pinch.
He got just halfway in his house
    And couldn't move an inch!

"What can I do?" poor Chipper cried.
    He really was upset,
Because, although his house was dry,
    Outside the world was WET.

"Maybe if I growl and jump
    And bark and wag my tail,
The other dogs will push me through
    Before it starts to hail!"

So Chipper made a lot of noise;
    He barked and howled and cried,
Until the dogs across the street
    Came running to his side.

"He's stuck! Hey, fellows, let's all pull!"
    The dogs began to shout;
And, grabbing Chipper's dripping tail,
    They tugged—and pulled him out.

Now Chipper plays the whole day long,
    He sits and dreams no more.
He'd rather bark and jump and run
    Than get stuck in his door.

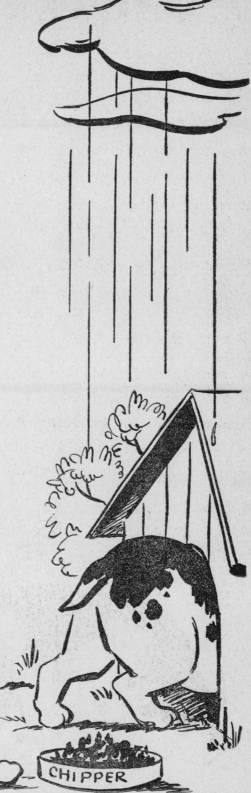

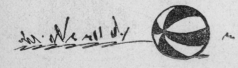

THE CIRCUS TRAIN

By Jessie M. Knittle

The circus train was speeding along,
Wrackity wrack, ding-ding-dong,
Racing through towns along the way
To Far Away City for Circus Day.
It puffed up the mountain and over the ridge;
It raced through the valley and over a bridge.
"Can't we go faster?" the manager cried.
And Brakeman O'Reilly stoutly replied,
"We're going as fast as our engine will."
When suddenly just at the foot of a hill,
The engine stopped! Yes, sirree!
Something had broken. What could it be?

The engineer and the brakeman, too,
Looked over the engine as trainmen do,
Trying to find what had broken so
The circus-train engine couldn't go.
Nothing was wrong with the boiler, it seemed,
For the circus-train engine still puffed and steamed.
There wasn't a hot box, a wheel wasn't flat—
What made the circus train stop like that?
Then they found that the driver had broken in two,
And they knew there was nothing that *they* could do.
The brakeman just shook his head in dismay.
"We'll have to stay right here today!
We'll have to wait for an engine to come
From Far Away City," he said, looking glum.

"Stay right here! Why, don't you know
At two o'clock we're to give a show
In Far Away City?" the manager fumed.
And the circus barker loudly boomed,
"Stay right here? In Village Small?
Why, you can hardly call *this* a village at all.
There's only one street, a church, and a store,
And very few houses, two dozen—no more!"
The elephants trumpeted, horses neighed,
And lions roared—such a racket they made!
Such a commotion and my, such noise!
For crowds of people and yelling boys
Came running to see the circus train
That had stopped and couldn't go again.

The circus performers were very provoked—
All but the clowns who laughed and joked.
The circus train manager tore his hair.
"We'll be late for our show, I do declare!"
Now Michael, who lives in Village Small,
Never had seen a circus at all.
"Since you can't give your show today
In the beautiful city of Far Away,
Please won't you have a circus here?"
And the tightrope walker standing near
Laughed to the circus acrobat,
"Ho-ho-ho. Did *you* hear that?
Give our show in *this* small town?"
"Let's do it. Let's do it," shouted a clown.
"Let's give them a show they'll *never* forget!"
"Let's *do!*" said the snake charmer Antoinette.

15

And Michael, why so delighted was he,
All he could say was, "Golly-gee!"
They pitched the tent by the railroad track,
And the circus performers began to unpack.

The circus barker yelled in the phone,
(You could almost hear the wires groan)
"Come to the circus in Village Small.
Stupendous! Colossal! Come one, come all!"

The postmen who traveled the rural routes
Blew on their horns the loudest *tooooooots*,
"A circus is coming to Village Small!
Fill up your wagons. Come one, come all!"

16

The Boy Scouts went from door to door.
They told all the people who came to the store.
They stopped the busses from other towns.
"Come to the circus and see the clowns!"

By circus time the tent was packed.
There wasn't an empty seat, in fact.
And Michael, who'd asked that they give the show,
Proudly sat in the very front row.
He cheered the circus acrobats,
The clowns on stilts with high top hats,
The lion trainer, the elephants, too!
And my, how sparkling his big eyes grew
When a trapeze artist fell in the net!
Indeed, 'twas a day he'll *never* forget.

The Grand Finale was almost through
When from far away came a low

WHOOOOOooo-WHOOOOOoo!

Then louder and louder, nearer it came.
The engineer from the circus train
Jumped to his feet and shouted loud
Above the noise of the band and crowd,
"The new engine's coming. Let's be on our way.
Remember, tomorrow's a Circus Day!"
Quickly the people filed outside.
"Here comes the engine!" Michael cried.
"It's come! It's coming far down the track!"
Too-too-tooooooooot, clackity-clack.
Quickly the circus crew took down the tent
And back in the cars all the animals went.
"You gave us a circus we'll *never* forget!"

18

Michael said to the clown and Antoinette.
And the circus performers all agreed
They'd enjoyed this day very much, indeed.
The shiny new engine from Far Away
Hooked onto the one that broke down that day.
Ding-dong-ding clanged the engine's bell,
And you should have heard all the people yell,
"Hurrah, hurrah for the circus train!"
Not even the manager could complain
'Cause the engine's driver had broken down,
For he'd had such fun in this little town.
He called to Michael from Village Small,
"We'll give you a show again, next fall."

Hucklebones

By Mickey Klar Marks

Hucklebones was a jolly young horse with very twinkly blue eyes and a velvety, black-and-white coat. He had a long white tail and a smooth white mane. He lived on a big farm in a comfortable, gray barn with a shiny weathervane on the top.

One beautiful morning when the sun was just lifting its sleepy eyes over the purple hills, Hucklebones saw the postman's rattly car stop at the mailbox near the gray barn. The postman dropped something into the mailbox and drove on down the road, *chug, chug, chuggety-chug.*

Hucklebones cantered eagerly over to the mailbox, clippety-clop, clippety-clop, and stood on his hind legs

and peered in. There, in the mailbox, was a big gray envelope. And will you believe it? Hucklebones's name was on the envelope. Yes, sir! It was addressed to—
Mr. Hucklebones, Esquire.

Hucklebones opened the letter and there, inside, was an invitation to the Steeplechase Ball, the biggest event of the year.

Hucklebones pranced happily back to the gray barn, tossing his mane and swishing his long tail. He couldn't wait to tell the others.

Suddenly Hucklebones stopped stock still in his tracks. A dreadful thought had come to him.

"Oh," he moaned. "Oh, dear! I won't be able to go to the Steeplechase Ball after all. They will dance the one-step and I don't know how. Oh, whatever shall I do? I wish someone would tell me what to do." And he sat down in the long green grass with his head on his front hoofs while the other animals roamed contentedly about the barnyard.

Hucklebones did know how to leap over a fence and he could gallop almost as fast as the wind.

He could canter around and around in a circle. He could trot down a hard paved road. He knew how to braid his long tail with red and purple ribbons. *But he didn't know how to dance a one-step.*

He could drink water from a pail without spotting his black-and-white coat. He could eat oats from a feed

bag. And he could eat hay from a feed box. *But he didn't know how to dance a one-step.*

He could carry a rider over hills and down into valleys and he could pull a wagon heavily loaded with eggs and milk and vegetables to the market in town. *But he didn't know how to dance a one-step.*

"Oh," said Hucklebones, "if I could only think of something to do about it. I do so want to go to the ball just once. How beautiful it must be to see all the horses—the big horses and the small ones, the brown horses and the black horses and the little spotted ponies, all of them dancing the one-step. It's the first time I've been invited and I can't go. I wish someone would tell me what to do!"

"Why, Hucklebones!" said a gentle voice. "You aren't your jolly self today. Whatever is wrong?"

Hucklebones turned to see kind old Mrs. Oo-ma, the cow, standing beside him.

"Oh," he sobbed. "I've been invited to the Steeplechase Ball."

"How wonderful!" said old Mrs. Oo-ma, gently. "But that should make you happy, and you are the saddest-looking horse I've ever seen."

"Yes, but I can't go," said Hucklebones.

And he put his head down on his hoofs again and sobbed aloud while Mrs. Oo-ma tried to think why he was sad about it.

Then he looked up at kind Mrs. Oo-ma and said, "You see there'll be dancing. I've heard the other horses tell about it. There'll be dancing, and they'll dance the one-step, and *I don't know how!*"

"There, there," mooed the kind old cow, soothingly. "There's a dancing school in the town. I've heard all about it. Why don't you go there? I'm sure they can teach you to dance."

"Why that's just what I shall do. It's an excellent idea," said Hucklebones, and he jumped up and cantered around Mrs. Oo-ma twice, just for luck. Then off he galloped, down the road and through the woods.

Down the hard paved road he trotted, clip-clop, clurkety-clickety, with his white mane waving in the morning breeze.

He trotted past the village church with its high pointed spire. Past the post office and the general store, clip-clop, clurkety-clickety until, at last, he reached the dancing school at the far end of the town.

Before Hucklebones went into the dancing school, he made certain that his beautiful white tail was straight and that his mane was lying smoothly along his neck.

Hucklebones was very happy as he entered the dancing school and saw the dancing class keeping time to the music—*tum, tum, tiddly, pom.* Around the room they danced and it was a beautiful sight.

But, alas, although the dancing teacher tried very hard and held Hucklebones's hoof and stepped in time to the music—*tum, tum, tiddly, pom*—Hucklebones could not do it. No, sir, he couldn't learn to dance the one-step.

He listened carefully to the tinkly tune the piano played. He watched the teacher as he stepped this way and that way. And he tried very hard to move each hoof separately, but Hucklebones just couldn't do it.

So back to the farm went Hucklebones. He didn't trot along the road. He didn't canter in a circle. And as for galloping through the woods—well, his heart just wasn't in it. What would he tell Mrs. Oo-ma?

As he walked slowly through the woods to the farm, his head was hanging low and his white mane completely covered his eyes. He didn't see a large rabbit come skittering out of the bushes on the left of the road that led to the farm.

"Halt!" shouted the rabbit in as big a voice as a rabbit can have, as Hucklebones stumbled sadly across the road.

"Watch those hoofs of yours. I'm moving my family to a new home. They are right behind me. Step carefully, please."

"Ulp!" Up went Hucklebones's head and back went his long mane.

"Oops!" he snorted in astonishment as he looked at the road swarming with rabbits.

There were rabbits everywhere. They scurried this way and that way, around Hucklebones's front hoofs and his back hoofs.

There were big rabbits and little rabbits, white rabbits and black rabbits and brown rabbits. There were gray rabbits and spotted rabbits, rabbits with pink eyes and rabbits with brown eyes. And each little rabbit had a soft, white cotton blob of a tail.

Very carefully Hucklebones lifted his left front hoof, then his right back hoof, then his right front hoof and his left back hoof. He stepped more carefully than he had ever stepped in his whole life because he didn't want to hurt any of the rabbits. Of course, you know that horses wear iron shoes and they are very heavy and hard.

One, two, three, four, went Hucklebones's hoofs—step-step, step-step. Suddenly his ears went up and

his eyes grew wide and his nose quivered wonderfully.

One, two, three, four.

"Step-step, step-step," he cried excitedly. "Why, I'm dancing. I'm really single-footing! *I'm doing a one-step!*"

And he really was dancing. In trying to avoid stepping on the rabbits, Hucklebones had learned to do what the dancing teacher could not teach him. Hucklebones had learned to dance the one-step. How wonderful!

Hucklebones never had felt jollier than he did at that moment. He waited until the last soft, white cotton blob of a tail has disappeared into the bushes, then off he galloped to the barn to tell Mrs. Oo-ma.

But now and then he stopped to practice, stepping -one, two, three, four—just to be sure he hadn't forgotten the steps.

When he reached the barn, he hurried to his stall where he was busy all afternoon.

He braided his tail with red and purple ribbons and he brushed his coat with a bristly brush. Then he combed his beautiful white mane until it was smooth and glossy. He polished his iron shoes until they glistened.

Then off he trotted to the Steeplechase Ball. Clip-clop, clurkety-clickety. Clippety-clop, clippety-clop.

Oh, how very wonderful it was! Hucklebones watched the graceful dancers—the big horses and the small ones, the brown horses and the black horses, and the little spotted ponies.

But I have it straight from Mrs. Oo-ma, who got it right from the mouth of the oldest horse at the ball, that the best one-step was done by Hucklebones. Yes, sir. There wasn't a doubt about it. Mr. Hucklebones, Esquire, was the best dancer at the Steeplechase Ball.

LET'S·GO·TO·THE·FAIR

By Mickey Klar Marks

I went to the Fair, oh, the grand County Fair,
With its noises and side shows and fun everywhere.
With so much to do and such odd things to see
I wished all day long there was much more of me.

"Guess your weight?" cried the man.
But he couldn't guess *mine*.
So I won a fat panda. Now wasn't that fine?

GUESS
YOUR WEIGHT

Along came a band with horns and a drum,
Marching and playing *te-tootle-boom-brum*.

I ate cotton candy all fluffy and pink;
It melts in your mouth and is gone in a wink.

I tossed one new penny, then two, then another,
Till I won a big vase to take home to my mother.

On the merry-go-round I rode a big horse
Pretending I was a real cowboy, of course.

Poultry and cattle, all shapes and all sizes,
Had come to the Fair to compete for the prizes.
There were many fat chickens—red, yellow, and white;
When I wanted to touch them, they cackled in fright.
One funny hen had a head like a mop.
A big rooster kept crowing; he just wouldn't stop.

A gray goose *honk-honked* like the horn of a car,
And the quacking of ducks could be heard from afar.

A blue-ribbon bull had a ring in his nose,
And the rope round his neck was as thick as a hose.

A small girl was leading a fat, jumpy calf;
How he kicked and bucked and made everyone laugh!

There were porkers and piglets penned in a field;
Some snorted or grunted but most of them squealed.

Inside a white tent, on long wooden tables,
Were pickles and jams and jellies with labels.
How I wished for a piece of the blueberry pie!
Or a slice of the cake that was three layers high!

The great orange pumpkin that won the first prize
Was so big it would make almost two hundred pies.

It made me so hungry I just had to run
And buy a big hot dog on a toasty brown bun.
But my arms were so full, when I started to eat,
The hot dog slipped out and fell down at my feet.

I bought me another and this time I found
My prizes were perfectly safe on the ground.

Some monkeys made faces but none of them pleasing;
I laughed, for I knew they all were just teasing.

The day turned to night and the stars came out, too.
There was so much to see I wasn't half through!

A clown with a face painted black, white, and red
Balanced a puppy dog right on his head.

A juggler tossed balls high up in the air.
I think he was the cleverest man in the Fair.

Then came a great noise——
     ZIP——RIP——BING, BANG, FIZ*zzz!*
Great firecrackers burst with a *whoosh* and a *whiz;*
They were shooting off rockets that turned the black night
Into a fairyland wondrous and bright.

I held out my arms and I stretched very far,
Trying to catch one shiny gold star.

It fell DOWN, down, down, but what would you suppose?
It burst!
   It went POP!
     Right in front of my nose!

When the last rocket burst, the band stopped its playing.
The crowd started homeward, all of them saying
The Fair had been grand. They were tired they said.
Why, even the chickens and lambs were in bed.

The Fair had been perfect, a barrel of fun,
I wished, how I wished, it had only begun!

I fell fast asleep and my wish *did* come true.
In my dreams there was so much to see and to do.
All the noises, the side shows, the people were there
In my dream of the Fair, oh, the grand County Fair.

the FLYING SUNBEAM

By D. N. Fairbairn

Alan's daddy was a pilot. He flew a big airplane with four engines and went to many foreign lands across the ocean. Alan liked to go to the airport with him and look at all the big airplanes. There were planes from England and France and Brazil and Holland and many other faraway countries. Each of them had a bright-colored flag of its nation on its rudder.

Alan always knew his daddy was going away on a trip when he put on his blue uniform with the gold stripes and buttons and the pretty gold wings. Mummy and Alan would help pack Daddy's big suitcase and they would all drive out to the airport.

At the airport Daddy would pick Alan up and give him a big hug and say, "Take good care of Mummy and be a good boy. I'll see you in a few days." Then he would climb the steps to the plane.

Alan always stayed to watch the engines start. He thought they must be very lazy because they sounded so cranky at first. But after a few minutes they always sounded more cheerful. Then the engines would roar with happy laughter as the plane began to move.

Alan and his Mummy waved as it moved away. It would come racing back along the runway and take off into the air.

A few days later the telephone would ring in Alan's house and Mummy would answer. Even when he couldn't hear what she said, Alan knew it was the airport because she sounded so happy.

"Daddy will be home today," she would say to Alan. Then they would both hurry to get ready so they would be at the airport when Daddy landed.

Alan always knew his daddy's plane when it circled to land because it had a big American flag on the rudder. Mummy and Alan would watch the landing to see that it was a smooth one. When it wasn't, Daddy had to buy them each an ice-cream soda. And if it was a good landing, he bought them each one anyway, to celebrate. That was fun.

One day Alan's daddy said to him, "How would you like to fly in an airplane? I know where we can go up in a tiny plane just big enough for you and me."

Alan was so surprised and happy he couldn't speak. He just nodded his head hard. And then he nodded again, just in case Daddy hadn't seen him the first time.

So Alan and his daddy drove to a little airport in the country. There were no runways there and no big planes. The field was all covered with grass and dotted with bright-colored little planes.

Alan and his daddy went into the hangar. Alan thought it was a big garage and that is really what it was. Only it was a garage for airplanes instead of cars. In one corner there was a man sitting at a desk.

Daddy said, "Hello, Charlie. Do you have a plane for me today?"

The man smiled at Alan, then he said to Daddy, "Well, that all depends. Are you Alan's daddy?"

Daddy smiled and Alan nodded hard.

"Yes," he told the man. "That is my daddy."

The man took them to a little airplane standing just outside the hangar.

"There you are," he said. "Will this one be all right?"

Alan smiled at the man. "Oh, yes," he said, "I like this one."

The little airplane was painted bright yellow. Alan thought it looked just like a sunbeam. So Daddy said, "All right. Let's call it Sunbeam."

Alan and his daddy climbed into the little seats and fastened their safety belts. Alan's daddy let him sit in front so he could see everything.

The man spun the little wooden propeller and the engine started. The plane began to move. The man waved good-by to Alan, and Alan waved back.

Daddy said, "When an airplane is moving along the ground like this, we call it taxiing."

Alan looked out the window at the hangars and the other planes. Just then he saw a long piece of cloth at the top of a pole. It looked like a great big stocking with the foot cut off.

"What is that?" he asked his daddy. "It looks like a sock."

"That is just what it is," said Daddy. "We call it a wind sock. It shows us which way the wind is blowing so that we will be sure to take off into the wind."

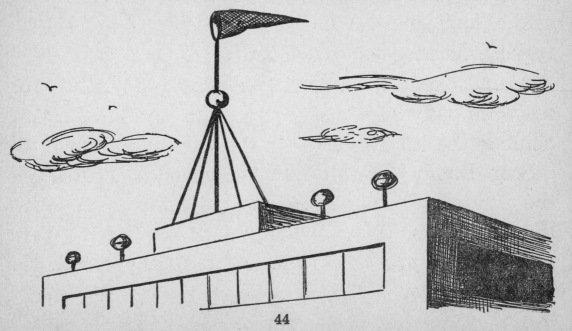

Just then Alan's daddy pushed on the brakes and Sunbeam stopped rolling.

"Are we going to take off now?" asked Alan.

"Not just yet," said his daddy. "We must warm up Sunbeam's engine to see that everything is working properly."

Daddy pushed the throttle forward and the little engine went faster and faster. Alan and his daddy listened to the engine. It sounded fine. Then Daddy checked the switches. Everything was all right. Sunbeam was ready to go.

Alan's daddy turned the little plane into the wind. He pushed the throttle all the way forward. The plane began to race across the field. Its tail lifted off the ground. It went faster and faster. Suddenly its wheels left the ground. The little plane was in the air!

Alan looked up at his daddy. Daddy smiled and said, "Sunbeam is flying well. Now we'll climb a little higher and then we'll fly over our house."

Alan looked out of the front window. All he could see were puffy little clouds in a blue sky while Daddy climbed the little plane.

Soon Daddy said, "We're two thousand feet above the ground. That is high enough for a little plane like Sunbeam. Now we'll fly over our house. Let's play a game and see if you can pick it out from the air before I do."

Alan laughed. "I bet I can," he said.

Alan looked out of the windows of the little plane. He looked very hard. He saw lakes and meadows and woods under the little plane. There were houses, too, but none that looked like Alan's and Daddy's. They looked like toy houses from up in the air.

Suddenly Alan saw a house with a red roof. *His* house had a red roof. The house had a white porch. *His* house had a white porch. Alan saw *his* sandbox.

"There's our house!" Alan cried.

Daddy banked the little plane over on its side.

"Why, so it is," he said. "You found it even before I did."

Alan saw a little figure run out of the house. It looked about as big as one of his toy soldiers. The little figure waved an apron at Sunbeam.

"Why, that's my mummy!" Alan thought. "How little she looks from up here!"

Alan's daddy waggled Sunbeam's wings so that Mummy would know they had seen her. Then he turned the little plane and started back to the airport.

Soon Daddy pulled the throttle back a little. Sunbeam's engine went slower and slower. They began to go down. Alan looked out and saw the airport.

Daddy said, "Now we must look at the wind sock again so that we'll be sure to land into the wind. That way Sunbeam will be going slower when we touch the ground and we can land very gently."

Alan's daddy turned the little plane into the wind and pulled the throttle all the way back. They began to glide toward the airport. The landing was so smooth that Alan didn't know they were on the ground until Sunbeam had nearly stopped.

Alan and his daddy taxied the little plane back to the hangar. When Alan jumped out he patted Sunbeam's yellow side.

"Sunbeam's a good little plane, isn't he, Daddy?"

"He certainly is," said Daddy. "After my next trip we must come here and fly together again. The next time I'll teach you how to fly Sunbeam yourself."

Alan was so excited he could hardly speak. "Wait until I tell Mummy," he said with a grin. "Won't she be surprised?"

MARCUS
By Alice Sankey

Once upon a time, Papa and Mamma Monkey lived in a little house deep in the jungle. They were both very proud of their little home. Mamma Monkey washed and ironed and sewed, and Papa Monkey hammered and sawed. He liked to work with tools and he made all sorts of work-saving gadgets for his little house.

He rigged up a movable trough and raised one end. Ripe coconuts rolled from the tree down the trough into his storage bin.

He attached a palm leaf to his hammock in such a way that as he swung gently to and fro the leaf would wave and fan him.

He even invented a special kind of cigar. It would snuff itself out after a few puffs, so one cigar would last all day, just like a lollipop.

Papa Monkey made a whole box of these cigars and had them ready to give to his jungle friends on the day his first child, a son, was born. When Papa Monkey saw his son for the first time he beamed at the cute little monkey snuggling in Mamma Monkey's arms.

"He looks like my Great-Uncle Marcus. He was a fine monkey. No one ever found fault with Great-Uncle Marcus. No one can find fault with this little monkey either. We shall name him after his Great-Great Uncle Marcus," Papa Monkey decided.

Papa Monkey picked up his cigars and rushed off to tell his jungle friends about his wonderful new son. He boasted that Marcus was the most perfect monkey ever born.

An old lion who was having trouble keeping his

cigar lighted, listened a while, then growled, "I have yet to see a perfect monkey."

"I shall be happy to show you my son," said Papa Monkey proudly, and he hurried home to have another look at Marcus.

As he came near his house, Papa Monkey heard loud sobs.

"Mamma is crying. I hope nothing has happened to Marcus," he said to himself, and hurried faster.

Marcus was lying in the hammock. He looked very sad. Mamma Monkey was standing in front of her washtub and tears ran down her cheeks and spattered into the soapy water.

"When I w-washed him and tried to hang him up by his tail to dry, it straightened out and he f-fell to the ground!" sobbed Mamma Monkey.

"Woe is me," moaned Papa Monkey. "A monkey with a straight tail. Who ever heard of such a thing!"

And he sat down and held his head in his hands.

"Don't cry, Mamma," Papa Monkey said finally. "We'll think of something." He got up and paced back and forth, back and forth.

Suddenly he snapped his fingers. "I have it! If Marcus's tail does not curl, *we'll curl it!*" he announced. He went to his workroom and poked around among his tools and gadgets.

He found some iron and some wood. He hammered

and pounded and twisted until he had made a curling iron. Then he picked up Marcus and carefully curled the little monkey's tail with his newest gadget. Mamma held her breath.

"See, Mamma?" Papa Monkey said proudly as he took the curling iron away. "Marcus's tail has a fine twirl at the end." Papa hugged the little monkey and took him to show his friends.

On the way, Papa Monkey had to pass the Baboon's Bakery Shop. Mr. Baboon had just put a huge cake with white icing out in front to show what good cakes he made.

"I will show you the advantages of hanging by your tail," Papa Monkey told Marcus. He scampered up the side of the building and climbed out on the sign hanging over the cake. He curled his tail around the bar from which the sign hung and reached down to scoop up some of the frosting with his finger. Marcus smacked his lips. The frosting looked good. He wanted to taste it, too.

"Now you try," Papa Monkey told Marcus.

Marcus scampered up the building just as his father had done. Marcus curled his tail around the bar. He clung to it with both hands. Then he let go with one hand. He let go with the other hand and cautiously let himself down. Marcus's tail behaved as no monkey's tail should ever behave. Instead of supporting him, it uncurled. It straightened. It slipped and let Marcus fall. *Slurp!*

Marcus fell! He fell right into the middle of the cake with white frosting. Papa Monkey groaned. He reached down and rescued his son. But Marcus left an outline of himself—a little monkey with a straight tail—right in the middle of Mr. Baboon's frosted cake. Papa Monkey carried him out of sight of the bakery and carefully licked off the frosting.

But Marcus began to whimper, "I want to hang by my tail, too."

"Don't cry, Marcus, we'll find something that will curl your tail," said Papa Monkey.

Papa Monkey went home and thought. The next morning he mixed a batch of thick starch. He dipped Marcus's tail into it and wound it around a bamboo pole. He told Marcus to sit very still. Papa and Mamma Monkey took turns fanning him until the starch was dry. Then Papa slipped the pole out of the tail. Sure enough! Marcus's tail had a beautiful curl.

Papa picked Marcus up and took him to show his jungle friends.

On the way they had to pass a section of road that was covered with fresh, wet cement.

"I'll show you the advantage of hanging by your tail," said Papa Monkey. "I'll climb out on the branch of that tree, reach down, and write my initials in the new pavement. Everyone will wonder how the initials got there. There will be no footprints leading to or away from them. Whoever passes will always be baffled, wondering how the initials got there."

"I want to baffle, too," said Marcus.

"Very well. You go first," said Papa Monkey.

Marcus walked along the branch until he was right over the wet pavement. Then he curled his starched tail around the branch. He clung with both hands. Then very carefully he let go with one hand. He let go with the other and cautiously let himself down.

Instead of clinging to the branch supporting him, as a monkey's tail should do, Marcus's tail uncurled. It straightened. It slipped and let Marcus fall. *Plop!*

Marcus fell right into the wet cement. Papa Monkey hurried out on the branch. He hung by his tail, reached down and pulled Marcus up into the tree. But in the wet cement Marcus left an imprint of a baby monkey with a straight tail. Papa Monkey shook Marcus until all the cement flew off. Marcus began to cry, "Oh, Papa, I want to hang by my tail!"

"Don't cry, Marcus. We'll think of something that will curl your tail," said Papa Monkey. He went home and thought and thought all the rest of the day.

The next morning Papa Monkey looked among his tools and gadgets. He found an old cane with a curved handle.

"I think this will bring you good luck," said Papa Monkey. "This cane once belonged to your Great-Great Uncle Marcus. You were named for him."

Papa Monkey tied the cane so that the handle formed a hook on Marcus's tail. When he was all ready, Papa Monkey picked him up and took him to show his jungle friends.

On the way they saw a big hippopotamus snoozing in the oozy mud.

"I will show you the advantage of hanging by your tail," said Papa Monkey.

He picked up a handful of pebbles and gave some to Marcus. Then he climbed into a tree near the hippopotamus and tossed a pebble. The big animal waggled his great head.

"I want to make him waggle, too," said Marcus.

Marcus hooked the cane end of his tail over the branch. He let go with one hand, then he let go with the other and cautiously let himself down. Before he could toss a single pebble, the cane slipped. It stayed hooked over the branch, but Marcus fell. *Splush!*

Marcus plopped right into the soft, oozy mud.

The hippopotamus began to wake up. He opened one eye and looked at the little monkey. Papa Monkey plucked Marcus out of the mud and whisked him away. The hippopotamus opened the other eye but all he saw was the imprint of the little monkey with a straight tail in the soft, oozy mud.

Papa Monkey took Marcus home. He was very sad.

"I give up," he told Mamma Monkey. "I fear Marcus will never hang by his tail."

Papa Monkey looked so sad and Mamma looked so

sad that Marcus decided to do something about his tail, himself.

He thought and thought and the next morning he poked among Papa's tools and gadgets and Mamma's sewing basket. He found a great big button and he had an idea. He fastened the button to the middle of his tail. Then he tied the end of the tail in a loop. Marcus went out to test his invention all by himself before he showed it to Mamma Monkey.

Marcus thought the Baboon's Bakery Shop was the best testing place. Mr. Baboon had just put a huge coconut-cream pie in front of the bakery, just where he had put the cake a few days before.

Marcus scampered up the building and out on the bar of the sign. He buttoned his tail around the bar. He let go with one hand. Then he let go with the other and cautiously let himself down. The button held fast! At last Marcus was hanging by his tail! How pleased Papa and Mamma Monkey would be! Then Marcus reached toward the pie.

Just then Mr. Baboon, who was kneading a big wad of dough, spied the little monkey reaching toward his pie. He ran out. Marcus saw him coming and tried to unbutton his tail, but he couldn't do it fast enough.

Mr. Baboon gave him a biff with the dough. Marcus held fast by the button, went twirling round and round, faster and faster and faster.

P O P ! The button flew into the air. *Squooosh!*

Marcus fell! He fell right into the middle of the coconut-cream pie!

Mr. Baboon plucked him out of the pie and marched him inside the bakery shop. He shook him so hard all the pie fell off.

Marcus began to cry. He cried and sobbed and cried. He cried so hard that Mr. Baboon became worried and gave Marcus a cookie to make him stop.

"Stop, stop!" cried Mr. Baboon. "I think you have learned your lesson. I'll not biff you any more!"

"But you would cry, too, if you were a little monkey and could not hang by your tail," sobbed Marcus.

Mr. Baboon looked thoughtful. This was serious.

"Did you try a curling iron?" he asked.

"Papa tried that, but it didn't work," said Marcus between his sobs.

"Did you try starch?" asked Mr. Baboon.

"Papa tried it but it didn't work," said Marcus.

"Did you try a cane with a curved handle?" asked Mr. Baboon.

"Papa tried it but it didn't work," said Marcus. "The button was my own idea."

"It's plain to see that didn't work," said Mr. Baboon. He looked sadly at his ruined coconut-cream pie.

"Maybe I can think of something," said Mr. Baboon, and he sat down and thought and thought.

"Have you thought of something?" asked Marcus after a few minutes.

"No. I should think your father would have figured out something by this time," Mr. Baboon said. "He is a clever monkey. He invented a pretzel-bender for me."

At that Mr. Baboon jumped up and threw his baker's hat in the air. "I have it!" he cried. "We will stick the end of your tail in the pretzel-bender!"

He took Marcus to the corner of the room where the pretzel-bender stood.

"Now, stand still for a few minutes," he said.

Marcus stood still for several minutes.

Then Mr. Baboon took out the tail and sprinkled it with salt just as he always salted his pretzels. Marcus's tail was curled. It not only had a curve to it; it had a half-pretzel twist inside the curve.

Mr. Baboon sprinkled Marcus's tail generously with salt and Marcus scampered toward home. He wanted

Papa Monkey to be with him when he tested his pretzel-bent tail.

As Marcus scampered through the trees he heard voices below him. An old lion growled, "When are you going to show us this perfect baby monkey?"

Marcus peeked through the leaves of the tree and saw the old lion below him talking to Papa Monkey. Papa looked very unhappy. He had made up his mind to tell his friends the truth. He would have to tell them that his son could not hang by his tail as a perfect monkey should. Just then Papa Monkey heard a noise in the branch over his head.

He looked up and could scarcely believe his eyes! Marcus's tail was around a branch. As Papa Monkey watched, Marcus let go with one hand, and then let go with the other. He cautiously let himself down.

Marcus was hanging by his tail! He waved both hands at Papa.

"Look, Papa, no hands!" he cried.

Papa Monkey's friends looked up, too.

"Gentlemen, my son!" said Papa proudly. His friends all clapped. The old lion growled.

"There's something funny about the end of his tail," the old lion said as he looked up at the monkey.

"I like the way it winds up," Papa Monkey said, laughing. Then he grasped perfect little Marcus, hugged him and whisked him away toward his home in the jungle.

Anna Marie

Up in the mountain and under a tree
Lives a little gray bunny named Anna Marie.
She lives all alone in warm weather and freezin',
With no one to speak to, and this is the reason:

Anna Marie never knew any rabbits.
(Her mother and father had wandering habits.)
She lived, when still young, by a clear little brook,
And never thought much of how bunnies should look,

Till rude Charley Chipmunk said, "My, you are queer!
You don't look a smidgin like me, you poor dear.
Your tail is too short and your ears are too long.
There's nothing about you that isn't all wrong."

Poor Anna Marie went next morning to look
At herself in the depths of the clear little brook.
"My ears *are* too long!" she exclaimed with a wail,
"And look at that queer little powder-puff tail!

I'm not like Sam Squirrel, or Red Fox, or Tom Cat,
I'm not like a chipmunk, a dog, or a rat.
I'm like nothing at all, and I'm going to hide
Where no one can laugh at my silly outside."

So hippity-hop went young Anna Marie
Up to the mountain and under a tree,
And there she lives yet,
    though she sometimes come down,
In the hour after supper, to visit the town.

If ever you're playing and happen to see
A little gray bunny, say, "Anna Marie,
Your tail is just right, and your ears are right, too,
And all of the bunnies in town look like you!"

TOMMY OF A-BAR-A RANCH

By Frances E. Wood

"Tommy, come here quick!" called his brother Bill excitedly. "Daisy has a new calf, and it's all white!"

Tommy ran with Bill to the small corral behind the cow barn. There stood Daisy, one of the milk cows, with one of the cutest calves Tommy had ever seen. Though it was only a few hours old, it looked at the boys with bright, interested eyes. When it took a few wobbly steps toward them, they laughed merrily at the comical way it walked.

"Just like a snowball on legs," Tommy said with a chuckle. "Hello, Snowball," he greeted the calf.

Tommy and Bill Jordan lived with their widowed mother in a small house on the A-Bar-A cattle ranch. Mrs. Jordan cooked for the cowboys, while Bill, who was nearly twelve years old, fed the chickens and calves and did other light chores. Nine-year-old Tommy followed Bill around and helped all he could, especially with the calves. Now, he fell instantly in love with the little newcomer.

When Mr. Anderson, the owner of A-Bar-A, came around the barn, he laughed at Tommy's rapt expression.

"So you like our new calf," he said, rumpling the little boy's hair affectionately.

"Oh, yes, Mr. Anderson!" answered Tommy happily. "Can we name her Snowball?"

Mr. Anderson thought that one over for a minute.

"Yes," he said at last. "That ought to be a pretty good name for her."

That evening, when the cowboys trooped into the kitchen and sat down at the long table, Bill and Tommy helped their mother carry in the food.

"Hi there, Shorty," called Steve, the foreman, who was Tommy's favorite cowboy. "I see you have a new calf to ride herd on."

"Yes," answered Tommy, setting down a big bowl of potatoes at Steve's plate. "Her name's Snowball."

"Snowball!" echoed another cowboy who liked to tease Tommy. "Aren't you afraid she'll melt, come the first hot day?"

Tommy laughed with the others at Stubby's joke. Then Slim spoke up, also bent on teasing. "She's kind of a puny little thing, ain't she?"

"She is not!" retorted Tommy. "She's a beautiful calf."

"That's right," said Steve. "The boss says she's the finest calf on the ranch."

After supper the boys followed Steve to the barn, where he went to fix the cinch on his saddle.

"I want to break a couple of broncs tomorrow," he explained. "Gotta get in practice for the rodeo next month."

"Oh, Steve, you don't need practice," said Tommy, loyally. "No old bronc can throw you."

Steve laughed and tweaked Tommy's nose.

"Thanks, Shorty," he said. "I hope you're right."

Then he asked Bill, "Are you going to enter the catch-it-calf contest? You'll win a calf, you know, if you rope and tie one in the contest."

"Gee, I'd like to," replied Bill, "but I haven't had any practice roping."

"Well, I reckon we can fix that," said Steve. "I'll show you how to handle a rope, and you can practice on the older calves in the north pasture."

"Oh, Steve," cried Tommy, "will you teach me, too? I'd like to catch a calf."

"You can practice with Bill," answered the cowboy, "but you're a little young for the contest. I'm afraid you'll have to be satisfied with taking care of Snowball this year."

"I'd like to have a calf of my very own," said Tommy wistfully. "Snowball is wonderful, but she belongs to Mr. Anderson."

The next evening Steve and the two boys took lariat ropes and went out to the north pasture where the cowboy showed Tommy and Bill how he coiled his rope, threw it over the head of a calf, and then threw and tied the calf. The way Steve did it, it looked easy, and Bill stepped up confidently and threw his rope at the calf. But, alas, it was not as easy as it looked. Bill's rope fell in the dust, and the calf romped away, kicking up his heels as if he thoroughly enjoyed the joke on Bill. Then Tommy tried his luck, but with no more success than his brother.

The boys practiced roping until almost dark, while Steve watched and offered suggestions. Finally, to Tommy's great delight, his rope settled down over the head of a big red and white calf, and the boy pulled the noose around its neck.

The calf gave a startled bawl and started on a gallop across the pasture, pulling Tommy along on the end of the rope, as Bill and Steve roared with laughter. Then it jerked the rope from Tommy's hands and went off, running and kicking and dragging the lariat until Steve and the boys caught it and removed the rope.

Every day for the next few weeks the two boys practiced roping the calves. Tommy, who was very quick, learned to rope his calf faster than Bill did, but he was never able to throw and tie it, as Bill learned to do. But Tommy kept trying, for he did so want a calf of his very own.

In the meantime, Snowball was growing fast. Tommy had taught her to drink from a bucket and was now taking almost the entire care of her. She seemed to think she belonged to him and ran to him whenever she saw him coming. When she rubbed her friendly little head against his shoulder, she almost consoled the boy for not being able to catch a calf of his own.

The night before the rodeo there was a cloudburst in the mountains above the ranch, and the next morning the little creek behind the corrals was a big, roaring stream.

"That creek is sure on a rampage," Mr. Anderson said to Steve at breakfast. "I hope none of the stock gets into it."

"Our stock is all safe," answered Steve, "but I don't know about our neighbors up the line."

"You'd better take the cowboys in the station wagon," Mr. Anderson said, "and stop at the Flying F ranch on your way to the rodeo. They might need some help. I'll take Mrs. Jordan and the two boys in my car."

The rodeo was being held at Wagon Wheel, twenty miles away. The catch-it-calf contest would be held in the morning, just before the free barbecue at noon, and the bucking contest would be in the afternoon.

While Bill and Tommy waited in the yard, Bill practiced with his rope. Just as he dropped a loop over the gatepost, Arthur Johnson, Bill's best friend, drove up with his parents.

"Going to the rodeo?" Arthur called to the boys.

"Oh, sure," answered Bill.

"Then come along with us," invited Arthur.

Mr. Anderson had come out of the house to talk to Mr. and Mrs. Johnson.

"Has the high water caused you any trouble?" he asked.

"It nearly got a couple of our calves," replied Mr. Johnson. "They fell into the creek, but we managed to get them out. It beats all how calves head straight for the water when the creek is flooded."

"Come on, boys," he added. "We'd better be on our way."

Mr. Anderson went back into the house, and Bill got into the Johnsons' car, but Tommy turned toward the corral.

"I'll go with Mother and Mr. Anderson," he called over his shoulder. "I want to be sure that Snowball is all right."

When he reached the calf corral, Tommy gave a little cry. A couple of poles in the fence were down, and several calves were outside. Evidently the storm had weakened the fence, and the calves had knocked down the poles.

"The fence looked all right this morning," Tommy said to himself. "One of the calves must have run against it after we fed them."

He looked around for Snowball and realized that she was nowhere to be seen.

"Snowball!" he called anxiously. "Where are you?" But no little white calf came running to meet him.

Hurriedly he drove the calves back into the corral and braced the poles into place as well as he could. Then he ran over to the creek and looked up and down it for Snowball.

At first he could see nothing. Suddenly, a short distance away, he saw something white in the water. When he got near enough to see what it was, his heart almost stopped beating. There in the stream, struggling to keep her head above water, was Snowball. She was wedged between a log and a sand bar, but the water was beating at her and threatening to wash her downstream at any minute. When she saw Tommy, she gave one feeble little bleat and struggled harder.

For an instant Tommy was paralyzed. Then he remembered his lariat hanging on the corral fence and ran to get it. Quickly he coiled it the way Steve had taught him, and threw it over the calf's head. Then he pulled it as tight as he dared and tied it securely to a nearby tree.

"There, little Snowball," he said encouragingly. "That will keep the water from carrying you away while I go for help. Now don't you worry. I'll be right back."

He ran as fast as he could to the house.

"Mother! Mr. Anderson!" he called, as he opened the door. But there was no answer. He ran through the house, calling as he went. Then he stopped short as he realized what had happened. Mr. Anderson and his mother, thinking he was with the Johnsons, had gone without him. There was no one to help him with Snowball!

Choking back his frightened sobs, he tried to think what to do. He wasn't very big, but neither was the calf, and she was depending on him to save her. So, back he went on the run.

The calf was lying quietly in the water, her head on the log. Tommy saw that she was getting weak and knew he would have to work fast. Making sure the rope was firmly tied to the tree, he waded out on the sand bar as near to the calf as he could. When he began to pull the rope, the frightened calf started to struggle frantically. Then she suddenly became quiet again and let Tommy drag her up to the sand bar, an inch at a time. When he finally got her into his arms, he found that she was not nearly so heavy as he had feared, and little by little, he managed to get her out of the creek and onto the bank.

He put her on the grass and sank down beside her for a moment. Then he noticed that the poor little calf was shivering. So, after rubbing her dry, he put a blanket over her, talking softly to her all of the time.

When she continued to shiver, he thought, "Maybe some warm milk would help."

While he was in the kitchen heating the milk, a car drove into the yard, and, to his joy, Tommy saw that it was Steve, driving Mr. Anderson's car.

"Hi, there, Shorty!" the cowboy greeted him. "What

do you mean, not coming to see me ride in the rodeo? You can't do that to me!"

Then he saw Tommy's face and knew that something was wrong.

"What happened, Shorty?" he asked gently.

For an instant the boy couldn't answer. The relief of having Steve appear so suddenly was almost too much for him. Finally he poured out his story. As he talked, he got the milk ready for Snowball, and he and Steve hurried out to her.

They found the calf a little stronger, and Steve carried her to the barn.

"As soon as she drinks this warm milk she'll be all right," he said encouragingly.

While they watched Snowball drink the milk, Steve explained, "When your mother found out you'd been left behind, I came back to get you. I told the boss I couldn't ride without Shorty to root for me."

Tommy giggled over that, then said, in alarm, "But you'll miss the contest."

"No, the bucking isn't until later this afternoon. We'll be there in time now that Snowball is all right."

When Tommy and Steve reached town, they learned that Bill had won his calf. Then the boys watched Steve win first place in the bucking contest.

That evening, when Mr. Anderson took them back to the ranch, he went first of all to the barn with Tommy to see about Snowball. She came running to meet them.

"I'm glad I couldn't enter the contest," he said to Mr. Anderson. "I'd rather take care of Snowball than have a calf of my own."

"You *do* have a calf of your own," said Mr. Anderson. "You have Snowball."

Tommy gave him a puzzled look. "But Snowball belongs to you," he said.

"No," said Mr. Anderson. "She belongs to *you*. When a boy takes as good care of a calf as you did of Snowball today, he deserves to have her for his very own."

And that is how Tommy won the finest calf on the A-Bar-A Ranch.

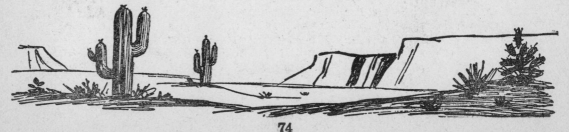

74

EGAN

By Alice Hanson

Egan was a little mouse as lively as could be.
The biggest thing about him was his curiosity.
    He loved to go exploring!

His father warned him, his mother, too.
His brothers and sisters (there were quite a few)
    Told him what not to do!

One night he was hungry; he couldn't sleep,
So out of his bed be began to creep
    Into the big, cold barn.

He smelled some bacon and toasted cheese.
His nose twitched so he began to sneeze,
    And his tail lashed up in surprise!

That moving tail touched a little spring
Which brought down at once a cold steel thing
    That almost crushed his tail.

How his family scolded; they all disapproved.
And father mouse said it was time they moved
For danger was much too near.

From Baby to Grandpa they moved out in a hurry,
And Farmer Brown thought he had one less worry
When he found that they had gone!

The mice never told him and he never knew
That they chose a new home, both clean and new
Right up in his attic!

When food was needed and Egan was sent
He always went down the cold air vent,
And he never had been caught.

One day in the kitchen he stared in dismay!
The farmer had spied him—he fled on his way,
And got halfway through the vent.

The farmer jumped up and caught Egan's tail.
But the mouse quickly turned around in his jail
And bit the man's finger!

That took lots of courage, don't think that it didn't!
The farmer withdrew his hand in a minute,
And Egan ran home.

He shivered and shook when telling about it.
But his bravery shone through——no one could doubt it!
His father and mother were pleased.

Here was a mouse who fought back at a man!
The bravest of brave in the whole mouse clan!
Over night he became a hero!

"I can't see what all the fuss is about,"
Thought Egan. Then he said with a shout,
"It had to be done——so I did it!"

PUSSY CAT'S Secret

By Mary Elting

"Where's Mr. Tuffy?" said Sue. "Here, kitty, kitty, kitty."

"Here, kitty, kitty," called John.

"He's disappeared again, I guess," said Willie James.

"Nice kitty," said Masha, the baby.

"He'd be nicer if he stayed at home," said Sue. "Oh, look. Here comes Daddy."

Sue and John and Willie James and Masha, the baby, ran to the gate to meet him. He put down his lunch box and gave them all a hug. Sue pulled his cap off and put it on her head.

"Are you going to be a fireman on a train like I am, Sue?" Daddy asked.

"Girls can't work for the railroad," said John.

"They may some day," said Daddy laughing, "but there aren't any girl firemen yet."

"Then I'll be the first one," said Sue. Daddy laughed and they all laughed.

They forgot all about Mr. Tuffy until Masha, the baby, said, "Nice kitty."

"Where's Mr. Tuffy?" Daddy asked.

"Mr. Tuffy's disappeared again," said Willie James.

"Did you look under the porch?" asked Daddy. They all nodded.

"Under all the beds?" Daddy asked. They all nodded.

"Everywhere?"

"Everywhere," said John sadly.

"I bet you didn't look in the old birdhouse up on the second limb of the apple tree," said Daddy.

So Daddy boosted Willie James up to look in the birdhouse.

But Mr. Tuffy wasn't there.

"Maybe he'll come home anyway," said Sue. "He always does."

"But where does he go?" asked John.

"It's a mystery," said Daddy. "Maybe you can solve it."

The next day Mr. Tuffy did come home. They were so glad to see him that they forgot to be cross.

"Meow," said Mr. Tuffy. And he went from one to another so they could all pet him and scratch him behind his ears.

"Let's give him some milk," said Sue. And they took him to the kitchen to get it.

But Mr. Tuffy wasn't hungry. He just sniffed the saucer and turned away.

He marched with his tail in the air to his basket by the stove and went to sleep very fast.

"You know what?" said Willie James. "We could be detectives and watch him every minute. We could even follow him the next time he goes away from the house."

"And that would solve the mystery of his whereabouts," said John.

So they began to watch Mr. Tuffy.

They watched Mr. Tuffy all the rest of the day. First Willie James watched, because he had had the idea. Then Sue watched and then John.

While John was watching, Willie James got some cardboard and tinfoil and cut out a detective's badge. After that, the one who was watching Mr. Tuffy wore the badge.

Mr. Tuffy woke up and ate a piece of liver for lunch. Then he had a busy afternoon. He chased a big fuzzy bee away from the nasturtium bed. He walked all around the top of the fence.

He thought he heard a mole under the grass and hunted all around the yard for it.

He climbed three trees.

Then he went to bed again. And everybody else was ready for bed, too, after following him all afternoon.

The next morning it was John's turn to watch Mr. Tuffy. He thought it was safe to sit down for breakfast with the others, because Mr. Tuffy was lying asleep in the dining-room window. But Sue, John, and Willie James soon had a contest to see who could eat the most pancakes, and John forgot to watch Mr. Tuffy. When he did look up again, Mr. Tuffy was gone.

"He can't be far away," said Sue. "Don't feel bad, John. It was our fault, too, for getting excited about the pancake contest."

John did feel very bad, however, and he handed the detective badge to Willie James to wear while they went outside looking for Mr. Tuffy.

When the postman came along, Sue asked, "Did you see our cat anywhere, Mr. Cohen?"

"Yes," said Mr. Cohen. "He was in front of the filling station."

So John and Sue and Willie James ran down to the filling station. Masha had to stay home. She was too small to follow.

"Kitty, kitty, kitty," they called as they hurried along the street. "Here, Mr. Tuffy."

The call boy was riding his bicycle along the street. He was going to wake up the railroad workers who might have slept too late. He called to the children. "Looking for your cat? I just saw him in front of Mr. Chang's store."

So Sue, John, and Willie James ran on to Mr. Chang's.

"Looking for that cat of yours?" said Mr. Chang. "I just saw him over at the railroad station."

So the three of them dashed over to the station and found Mr. Pulaski, the station agent.

"Oh, Mr. Pulaski," said Sue, "have you seen our cat?"

"Is he a pepper-and-salt kind with white feet? I've seen one like that around here lately."

"Oh, yes, that's Mr. Tuffy!" said John. "We've solved the mystery."

"No," said Willie James, "we haven't. Not until we really find him here." So the three of them sat down on a baggage truck to think of some plan for finding Mr. Tuffy.

They finally decided to take turns watching the railroad station for Mr. Tuffy.

"No, I don't mind," Mr. Pulaski said when they asked him, "because you're railroading children and have sense enough to stay off the tracks and not get in anybody's way."

Willie James was the first one to watch, while Sue and John went home to tell Mother about their plan.

When Sue came back she carried a knapsack. In it she had some peanut brittle for herself, a chocolate bar for John, and there were some sliced carrots for Willie James because he liked them better than candy. There was also a pillow to sit on when they were tired from watching for Mr. Tuffy. And, of course, there was a piece of herring for Mr. Tuffy in case they found him.

"Maybe if we put the herring where Mr. Tuffy could smell it, we could catch him," said Willie James.

They cut the herring in two small pieces. One piece they put near the scales that stood beside the baggage-room door. They put the other piece underneath the platform where the trains unloaded the express packages.

It was John's turn to watch for Mr. Tuffy. He kept looking from one piece of herring to the other until he heard the put-put of a handcar behind him.

It was the handcar that the section crew used when they went out to fix the tracks. Railroad people called the section crew the "gandy dancers." John waved at them. Then he looked back just in time to see a white paw from under the express platform snatch the herring.

"Here, kitty, kitty, kitty," John called, and he dashed over to the platform.

"Where is he?" Sue cried as she came running up. John pointed, and they both bent down to look under the loading platform. There was a cat eating the herring, but it wasn't Mr. Tuffy!

"We have only one piece of herring left," said Sue. "I guess I'll just have to sit close to it."

So Sue sat near the baggage room all afternoon.

She ate her peanut brittle. No more cats came near the station. At dinner time she had to go home.

The next morning was Willie James's time to watch. He had a good idea. He cut the piece of herring in two and tied a string to each half. Then he put the ends of the string under the pillow and sat on them. That way the wrong cat couldn't run off with the fish.

Willie James sat and sat, eating his carrots. After a while Mr. Stone came over to him. Mr. Stone was the guard who let down the big gates to stop automobiles from crossing the tracks when a train passed.

"Hello," said Mr. Stone. "Do you work for the railroad, too?"

"Well, sort of," said Willie James.

"I hear that baby sister of yours is getting big enough to swing a banjo." A banjo is what firemen on a train call their shovel. "You're sure enough a

railroading family," Mr. Stone said, smiling broadly.

"Um-hum," said Willie James. "A railroading family." And then he had another idea. He thought he knew where Mr. Tuffy had gone!

Willie James hurried in to ask Mr. Pulaski, the station agent, whether the Yankee-Doodle Flyer was going to be on time.

"Yes, siree," said Mr. Pulaski. "In about thirteen minutes she'll be here."

Then Willie James asked permission to use the telephone. He called Sue and John and told them to come down to the station at once.

They hurried down to the station and arrived just as the Yankee-Doodle Flyer was pulling in.

"Where's Mr. Tuffy? Where is he?" Sue and John both shouted as they ran up to Willie James.

"Come on," said Willie James. He ran down the platform to the place where the Yankee-Doodle's dining car had just stopped.

"Where are we going? Where is Mr. Tuffy?" Sue and John kept asking. "Why did you call?"

Willie James just pointed. The side door of the dining car opened and what do you think they saw?

There was a cook getting off with a big pail of garbage. And right behind him, hopping down the steps, came Mr. Tuffy.

Sue ran and picked him up. Mr. Tuffy began to purr.

The cook looked surprised. "That your pussy?" he asked.

"Oh, yes," said Sue.

"Well, well," laughed the cook. "But he's part Yankee-Doodle cat, too. He makes the run with us mighty near every time.

"He's waiting here to be picked up when we go

west, and we let him off when we come back."

"And that's why he's not hungry when he comes home," said Sue. "Shame on you, Mr. Tuffy." But she hugged him anyway.

"How did you know where to find Mr. Tuffy?" John asked Willie James.

"I didn't know," said Willie James. "I just guessed when Mr. Stone said we were a railroading family. I figured we might have a railroading cat, too. Daddy told us about a dog named Owney that used to ride trains all over, remember?"

So Sue, John, and Willie James started home. They took turns carrying Mr. Tuffy. They didn't want to lose him again.

When they passed Mr. Chang's store, they stopped to tell him all about solving the mystery of Mr. Tuffy's disappearance.

"Well, well, well," said Mr. Chang. "You certainly are good detectives."

In the next block they met the call boy. They had to stop and tell him all about Mr. Tuffy and his ride on the Yankee-Doodle Flyer.

"That sure is a queer cat," the call boy said, and he hopped on his bicycle and rode down the street.

At their gate, they met the postman and told him about Mr. Tuffy's trip.

"You're pretty good detectives," the postman said, laughing.

When they went into the house, they told Mother about Mr. Tuffy's travels. Masha, the baby, laughed and patted Mr. Tuffy. "Nice kitty," she said.

And Mother, Sue, John, and Willie James agreed that Mr. Tuffy was the nicest kitty, even though he liked to travel.

Fluff

Fluff was a little yellow kitten who lived with the Whites. Every morning Mother Tabby me-owed and me-owed for her.

"Now you take your kittenbath," scolded Mother Tabby. "You know you have a special kind of tongue for it, Fluff. It is as rough as a hairbrush and keeps your fur pretty and shiny."

Fluff scowled. Her pink tongue was *so* tiny. Besides, she even hated the word BATH. It made her think of water—and how she hated water!

It made her think of the time she spilled the drinking bowl and got her paws just soaking wet.

One morning Fluff decided she just wouldn't take her kittenbath.

She hid behind the big broom until Mother Tabby stopped calling.

Then she waited until the outer door opened. She scooted out just as fast as she could!

Fluff went so fast that she skidded across the porch, tumbled down the steps, and—SPLASH! She landed in a mud puddle.

She scrambled to the edge, for she SO hated water!

But when she was out of the puddle, she got wetter and wetter, for rain was coming down hard.

Poor Fluff! Instead of looking like a fluffy, yellow kitten, she looked like a mud pie!

WOOFUS

By Jane Curry

This is the story of Woofus, a smooth little black-haired puppy who grew up to be a great big woolly dog.

Woofus's brothers and sisters were golden-brown puppies, and Woofus was disappointed that he was black and not brown like the rest of the family.

When visitors came down to the kennel with Bobbie and Jean to look at the puppies, they would say, "Aren't those cute little puppies! But, oh, look at that funny little black one."

And Woofus would hang his head. He knew they were laughing because he was black and not brown like his brothers and sisters.

People always asked why the little black puppy was named Woofus. It seemed like such a silly name.

Well, really, Woofus named himself. When the other puppies would bark, "Bow-wow," Woofus always said, "Woof-woof." Bobbie and Jean decided that Woofus was a fine name for a puppy that said, "Woof-woof."

One day Bobbie and Jean tied red ribbons on all the brown puppies and carried them away to new homes.

"Hm-m," Woofus thought to himself. "I guess no one wants me. But I will be a great big brave dog and Bobbie and Jean and their mother and daddy will be glad they kept me."

As the weeks passed, Woofus grew bigger and bigger. And strange as it may seem, his black coat got longer and woollier. One day when Bobbie and Jean came down to the kennel with their mother, they laughed and laughed and laughed because Woofus looked as though he had on a woolly bonnet and woolly stockings.

You couldn't fool Woofus. He knew they were laughing at him, and he said to himself, "People laugh at me now, but some day I will not only be a big brave dog, but I will be a big handsome woolly dog." All he said to Bobbie and Jean and their mother was, "Woof-woof."

But they just laughed because he did look very funny with his woolly bonnet and woolly stockings.

Woofus was right. He did grow up to be a great big woolly dog. But still people laughed at him. When they laughed he would just put back his head and cry "Woof-woof." If you can understand dog language you must know that Woofus was saying, "I may be a funny dog, but I am a big dog and a woolly dog and I am surely going to be a brave dog. Some day Bobbie and Jean and their mother and daddy are going to be proud of me. They are going to be glad they kept me for their dog."

One evening Bobbie's and Jean's daddy came home and said, "How would you children like to go on a picnic tomorrow?"

"Goody, goody!" exclaimed Bobbie and Jean. "We'll take our supper and go to the woods. And, oh, Daddy, may we take Woofus?"

Daddy decided that Woofus might go, because he was getting too big to be kept fenced in all the time.

So the next day Bobbie and Jean helped their mother make sandwiches and pack the picnic basket. Everything looked so good that they could hardly wait to get started for the woods.

Now Woofus had never been to the woods and he was so excited he could hardly keep quiet a minute. The buzz of the bees and the cheeps and chirps of the squirrels and chipmunks had him dashing wildly back and forth, barking, "Woof-woof."

Bobbie and Jean and Daddy and Mother laughed and

laughed, because Woofus acted like such a silly dog. All of a sudden they noticed that he wasn't running around but was standing at the foot of a tree woofing as loudly as he could.

Bobbie ran over to see what the trouble was. He couldn't see anything, and he scolded Woofus for making such a disturbance. But Woofus kept on woofing. Then Bobbie heard a weak little "Me-ow" from the treetop. Sure enough, there was a little black kitten peeking through the leaves.

"Mother, Daddy, Jean," Bobbie called, "see the little black kitten Woofus has found."

They were all much surprised. Daddy said he would get the little kitten down from the treetop if they would take Woofus away.

Mother and Daddy decided that Bobbie and Jean might take the little lost kitten home.

"But what about Woofus?" asked Bobbie. "Do you think he will like the kitten?"

"Woofus is a very smart dog," said Daddy, "and I think that because he discovered the little black kitten they may become very good friends."

"What can we name the kitten?" asked Jean.

"Yes, what would sound well with Woofus?" asked Mother.

"How about Goofus?" asked Daddy.

"Oh, no," said Mother.

"Oh, no," said Bobbie.

"Oh, no," said Jean.

"I know," said Bobbie. "Let's call him Tar Baby because he is as black as tar."

And Mother, Daddy, and Jean agreed that Tar Baby was a good name for the little black kitten that Woofus had found.

Woofus really wasn't much pleased to have Bobbie and Jean bring Tar Baby home with them.

Tar Baby could climb trees and fences and run up into the house, and Woofus, being a dog, had to stay in his own private dog yard. And while Woofus was sitting in his dog yard thinking, as he quite often did, Tar Baby would be frisking on the fence above his head.

Woofus would close his eyes and dream of the things he might do so that he would not only be a big dog and a woolly dog, but a very brave dog. Right in the middle of his dream Woofus would bark, "Woof-woof!" Poor little Tar Baby would be very frightened and stand up ready to jump off the fence. But Tar Baby never had to jump, because Woofus would just sigh and dream on.

Bobbie and Jean worried because Woofus and Tar Baby did not become better friends. But Daddy said to give them time because Woofus was really a smart dog.

And Daddy also thought that it would be a good idea to let Woofus out of his yard more often, because he was such a big dog and, Daddy thought, a good dog, too.

One night there was a storm and the wind blew the rain, and there was thunder and lightning.

"Poor Woofus," said Bobbie, looking up at the rain running down the windowpane.

"Poor Tar Baby," said Jean, sitting up in bed and looking at the window, too.

They could hear Woofus bark, "Woof-woof," and then Tar Baby would cry, "Me-ow, me-ow."

"I wonder if they are getting wet," said Bobbie. Jean wondered, too. So imagine their surprise the next morning when they went to the kennel and saw—

Woofus and Tar Baby cuddled up close together in Woofus's dog house!

"My goodness," said Bobbie.

"My goodness," said Jean.

Then Woofus woofed and woofed and Bobbie and Jean knew that he was telling them that he and Tar Baby were friends.

Later in the day Daddy had a painter put Tar Baby's name on the dog house with "Woofus." Bobbie and Jean were very pleased.

Tar Baby was pleased. Woofus was pleased, too. He said to himself, "I am a big dog. I am a woolly dog, and I am a smart dog. But I must be good and brave so that Bobbie and Jean will always be glad they kept me."

But poor Woofus! He forgot that he must always be a good dog.

The next morning Mrs. Jones, a neighbor, telephoned and said, "Woofus has ruined my vegetable garden."

"Oh, dear, oh, dear," said Mother. "Are you sure it was Woofus who did it? He is always such a good dog."

But Mrs. Jones was sure it was Woofus and no other dog.

That afternoon the telephone rang again. This time it was Mrs. Smith. Woofus had pulled her clean clothes off the line and dragged them in the dirt.

"Oh, dear, oh, dear," said Mother. "Are you sure Woofus did it? He is such a good dog."

But Mrs. Smith was sure.

So Bobbie scolded Woofus and Jean scolded Woofus and Mother scolded Woofus and Daddy scolded Woofus.

Woofus hung his head in shame and said to himself:

"I am a big dog and a woolly dog. I am a smart dog. I must be a good dog. I must be a brave dog, too."

"Where is Woofus?" asked Bobbie and Jean the next afternoon.

"Where is Woofus?" asked Mother.

Tar Baby was sitting in the kennel yard all alone and neither purring nor looking happy. And Woofus —well, they called and called, and he was nowhere to be found.

Woofus didn't come home for supper, and the family was very sad.

While they were eating, the telephone rang.

"There's the telephone," said Mother. "Maybe someone has found Woofus."

They all waited anxiously.

"Why, what do you think?" said Mother when she came back. "Tommy Jones fell in the creek and Woofus jumped in and pulled him out and saved him. So Mrs. Jones is not angry about her vegetable garden any more."

"I wish Woofus would come home," said Bobbie and Jean.

Just then the telephone rang again.

"It was Mrs. Smith," said Mother. "She says Woofus is a very brave dog to rescue Tommy Jones from the creek. She is not angry about her wash being pulled off the line now."

"I wish Woofus would come home," said Bobbie and Jean.

When Woofus did come, there was a very special big bone in honor of his bravery. Tar Baby didn't try to get even a smell of it. He just sat and watched Woofus and purred.

Bobbie and Jean came down to the kennel to tell Woofus what a good, brave dog he was, and how proud they were to have him, and he said, "Woof-woof—woof. Woof-woof."

In dog language that means, "I am a big dog and I am a woolly dog. I am a smart dog and I try to be a good dog. Now I know I am a brave dog." Then he went on chewing his very special big bone.

What Happened to FLUFFY?

By Virginia Cunningham

Fluffy was the softest, fluffiest little black kitten that ever was. That is why Jill named her Fluffy. All day long every day Fluffy and Jill played together as happy as could be.

But one day Jill said, "Here, Fluffy. Come get in your basket. Don't you know we're going to move today? You're going on the train with us."

Fluffy scampered behind the evergreen bushes and peeked out at Jill. But she didn't jump in her basket. She ran off across the yard after a butterfly.

"All right," Jill said. "I won't put you in your basket till the last minute."

Then Jill tied a spool on a string and ran off across the yard dragging it behind her.

Jump! Fluffy pounced on the string. Jill jerked it away and started running again. Off went the kitten after her.

All of a sudden Fluffy stopped short and crouched against the ground. Then—jump! She landed with her paws right on the spool. She rolled over and over until she was all tangled up in the string.

Just then Jill's mother came to the door.

"Jill," she called. "Come put your hat and coat on. Father will be here soon with the taxi to take us to the train, and we must be ready."

Then Mother looked around the yard. "Where is Ted?" she asked with a worried frown. "I declare, that brother of yours doesn't stay put two minutes."

"He went to the dime store," Jill said. "Mrs. Brown gave us each a dime. She said it was a going-away present because we are moving out of town. See, I have my dime in my pocket."

"Dear me," Mother said, "I hope he comes right back. Put on your hat and coat and then watch for him. When you see him coming tell him to hurry."

Then Mother went off to see about the moving men. They had backed a truck up to the side door and were carrying out all the furniture. By the time the family reached their new home, all the furniture would be there, too.

"Don't forget the porch furniture," Mother told the men, and they promised they would remember it.

Pretty soon Jill saw Ted coming up the street.

"Hurry, Ted," she called. "Mother wants you."

Ted came running. "Look, Jill," he said. "Look what I bought at the dime store. A magic bubble blower!"

Ted puffed on the bubble blower and out floated shiny, round soap bubbles. Blue, red, green and silver —all sparkling in the sunlight.

Fluffy stopped playing with the string and began watching the bubbles. She cocked her head first on one side and then on the other. What are those pretty round things, she seemed to say.

Fluffy put out her paw to touch one. Pouf! It disappeared.

Fluffy looked so surprised that Jill and Ted burst out laughing.

Ted blew more bubbles just as fast as he could. The bubbles went sailing through the air straight toward Fluffy. Fluffy leaped to catch them. One minute there

were a lot of bubbles, and the next minute there weren't any. Fluffy just couldn't understand what had happened to all the bubbles.

One big bubble floated over toward the porch chair, and Fluffy chased it. The bubble caught against the rocker but it did not burst.

Fluffy crouched low. Slowly, slowly she stretched out her nose to sniff at the strange round thing. The minute she touched it, pouf! It disappeared.

Ted blew more bubbles, a great cloud of them. Fluffy chased each one. One floated into the pocket on the arm of the wicker rocker. Fluffy dived in after it.

Just then Jill saw the taxi and ran to call her mother.

The moving men hustled the last of the furniture into the truck and drove off.

Father got out of the taxi and told the driver to wait. Then he went to help Mother.

"Is everybody ready?" he asked.

"Everybody but Fluffy," Jill said. "I waited till the last minute to put her into her traveling basket."

"Well, this is the last minute," Father said. "We have just barely time to catch our train."

"Here, Fluffy," Jill called.

But no little black cat came to answer her. Jill called again. Then Ted called. They looked all over the yard. They looked all over the house—upstairs and down. No Fluffy.

Father stood by the taxi with his watch in his hand. Mother helped the children look for Fluffy. In the rose garden. Behind the evergreen shrubs. Under the lilac bush. No Fluffy. There were fluffy gray pussies on the pussywillow bush, but there wasn't a live pussycat, not anywhere.

What had happened to Fluffy?

"We'll have to go without her," Father said at last. "The train won't wait."

Mrs. Brown came out of her house next door to ask what the matter was.

"I'll find Fluffy," she said. "Don't you worry. I'll find her and send her to you on the next train."

"Fine. Thanks," said Father, and he lifted Jill into the taxi before she could say a word.

The taxi whirled off down the street and reached the station just in time.

The conductor was standing by the train steps.

"All-ll abo-oard," he called.

"Hold it!" yelled Father, and they all raced pell-mell through the station.

Father had hold of Jill's hand, and he made her go so fast that she felt as if she were flying.

Up the train steps she went, with Ted right behind her. Then came Mother and Father.

"All aboard," called the conductor again, and he gave the signal to start the train.

For a few minutes Jill was so busy catching her breath that she almost forgot about Fluffy. But soon she was thinking about her again. What had happened to Fluffy?

"The last time I saw Fluffy," Jill said, "she was jumping up on the porch rocker after a bubble."

"That's the last time I saw her, too," Ted said gloomily. "Maybe that's the last time we'll ever see her."

"Stop worrying," Father said. "Mrs. Brown will take good care of her."

Jill stopped talking about Fluffy, but she did not stop worrying about her. What if Mrs. Brown did not find her?

But soon there were so many things to see from the train windows that Jill did stop thinking about the lost cat.

After a while the conductor came into the car. "All change here," he said.

Everyone got off and went into the station.

The family had to wait in the station quite a while. But at last their train came and they climbed aboard. In a few hours their journey was over.

"Here we are," Father said. "This is the town where we are going to live."

Then he beckoned to a taxi driver and told him where they wanted to go.

"There's the post office," called Ted as the taxi

went down the main street. "There's a church. There's a school."

Jill wished he would say, "There is Fluffy." But of course he didn't.

At last the taxi turned onto a wide street with trees on both sides.

"There's our new home," Father said. "That white house on the corner."

Jill and Ted leaned forward to look, and Ted called excitedly, "There's the moving van. See. It beat us here."

"No wonder," Mother said. "We had a poky old train and that long wait in the station."

Jill and Ted jumped out of the taxi and ran across the grass. They ran all around their new house.

Mother was talking to the moving men. "Bring out the porch furniture first," she said. "Then at least our porch will look like home."

"Okay, ma'am," said the men. First they took out a table and chair, then the big rocker.

Of course the rocker made Jill think of Fluffy. She could almost imagine she saw the little black cat crouching in the pocket on the arm of the chair.

All of a sudden Jill blinked her eyes. Was she imagining it, or was that fluffy black spot in the pocket really Fluffy?

"Meow!" said the fluffy black spot. "Meow!"

And out scrambled Fluffy.

The men were so surprised that they dropped the chair with a bang.

Jill raced across the grass and gathered Fluffy into her arms. "Fluffy, Fluffy," she said over and over.

"Purr-rr, purr-rr," answered the little black cat.

Ted had to hug Fluffy, too. So did Mother and Father. Fluffy purred louder and louder.

"Well," Father said, "so that's what happened to Fluffy."

The moving men scratched their heads in surprise. "And to think she rode all the way with us in the truck and never made a sound."

"Meow! Meow!" said Fluffy in a complaining tone. "*Meow!* MEOW!"

Jill laughed. "She's certainly making a sound now. I guess she's hungry."

Mother thought a moment. "Let me see," she said. Then she nodded her head. "Find a big green wooden box," she told the movers. "There's canned milk in the big green box."

The movers dragged out the green box, and soon Mother had the can of milk open.

Mother bent the lid way back so that Fluffy would not hurt herself on the rough edges.

All the time Mother was fixing the milk, Fluffy rubbed against her ankles and purred happily.

"She knows that's for her," Jill said.

Lap, lap, lap went Fluffy's little pink tongue. Soon the milk was all gone.

Fluffy sat up and washed her face and paws daintily.

Meantime, the movers had been bringing in the furniture.

Mother, Father, Ted, and Jill all helped put things in place.

As Jill was unpacking her dolls, Fluffy came bounding across the floor. The little cat began to sniff at each doll.

"Meow," she said in a disappointed tone.

Then Fluffy went out into the hall. She went into each room and sniffed at everything she saw.

She sniffed at chairs and tables.

She sniffed at Father's fishing pole.

She sniffed at Ted's ball glove.

She sniffed at Ted's butterfly net, too. Bang! Down it came on top of her.

"Me-ow-owr!" yelled Fluffy inside the net. She tried to run away, but the net came right with her.

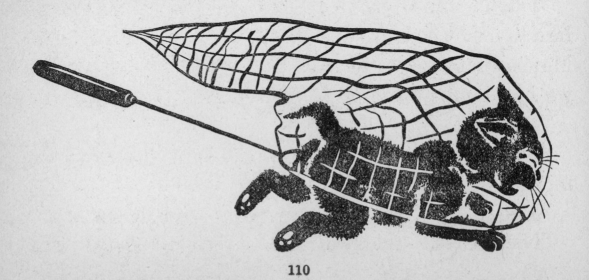

Jill came running to help her. As soon as Fluffy was out of the net, she ran out of the house as fast as she could go.

In a few minutes Jill heard Fluffy meowing again.

"Fluffy, Fluffy," Jill called. "Where are you?"

"Here she is," called one of the movers. "She's in the truck."

Jill called and called, but Fluffy would not come out of the truck.

Jill ran to her mother. "Oh, Mother," she said. "What is the matter with Fluffy? Doesn't she like our new house? All she does is sit in the truck and meow."

Mother went to the window and watched Fluffy for a moment. The little cat kept on meowing. When she wasn't meowing she was sniffing at something in the back of the truck.

"Oh, dear," Jill said. "What is the matter with her?"

"I don't know," Mother said. "But most cats don't like to move. They like to have a home and stay there. Maybe Fluffy wants to go back to our old house. Maybe we had better give her to the people who bought it."

"Oh, no," Jill cried.

She ran out to the van and picked up the little cat in her arms.

"Meow," said Fluffy, and tried to squirm away.

"Nice kitty," said Jill softly. "Pretty kitty." She

began to stroke gently the cat's soft fluffy fur.

Fluffy quieted down and began to purr.

"You don't want to leave me, do you?" said Jill. "This is our house now. See, here are all our things."

Jill carried Fluffy all over the new house and showed her the old furniture so that the cat would feel at home.

"There now," said Jill at last. "I've showed you everything. Don't you feel at home?"

"Meow-owr!" said Fluffy. She didn't sound as if she felt at home. She sounded very unhappy.

She jumped out of Jill's arms and ran straight back to the moving van.

All of a sudden Jill knew what was wrong.

"Fluffy wants her bed," Jill cried. "Where's her bed? It must be in the moving van."

The moving men shook their heads.

"No bed here," they said. "Everything is out except this dollhouse."

"That's it," cried Jill, and clapped her hands. "Fluffy has slept in my dollhouse ever since she was a tiny kitten."

So the men carried the dollhouse up to Jill's room, and Fluffy followed them.

She wasn't meowing now. She was purring as loud as a sewing machine.

Jill patted Fluffy's pillow till it was nice and smooth. The little cat crawled into her house and curled up on the pillow with her paws tucked under her chin.

"There," declared Jill happily. "There's your house, Fluffy. You didn't move out of it. It came right along with you. You can live in your old house and in our new house at the same time. We won't have to send you back after all."

"Purr-rr, purr-rr, purr-rr," said Fluffy, and she looked as if she were the happiest, most contented cat in the whole world.

MEE, RAY, DOH!

Mee, Ray, Doh!
Pussy's in the snow;
Back she comes, oh, what a sight,
Wearing little boots of white;
Jimminy, oh, Jimminy, oh, Jimminy, oh, Jo!
Mee, Ray, Doh!
Where shall pussy go?
By the fire she shall remain,
Lick her stockings clean again;
Jimminy, oh, Jimminy, oh, Jimminy, oh, Jo!

WILLIE THE LIGHTHOUSE

By Mary Johnson

Willie was a very small lighthouse. He stood on top of a high hill overlooking the big blue ocean.

Everyone had forgotten Willie, except Mr. Pennyfeather. How could *he* forget Willie when he lived inside of him!

But Mr. Pennyfeather was worried. Every month he sent a letter to Washington, D. C. asking if Willie couldn't have a new light, a little fresh paint, and maybe a big new rescue boat. Every month a letter came back from Washington saying that Willie was too old and too little to bother about.

The last letter from Washington had said that in a month Mr. Pennyfeather would have to move out! No one was going to live in Willie any more! Mr. Pennyfeather was sad, because he and Willie had become good friends.

Mr. Pennyfeather was sure that Willie understood the last letter because he began to look sadder and *sadder* and SADDER! His paint started to peel off and his light became dimmer and dimmer. Some nights it almost didn't go on at all!

One night Mr. Pennyfeather was having a particularly hard time coaxing Willie's light to go on. It was dark and the fog was thickening. The waves were as tall as Mr. Pennyfeather and were growing taller every minute. Soon they were splashing Willie himself!

Mr. Pennyfeather tried and tried but the light just wouldn't budge. He knew Willie was trying, too, but Willie was old and tired and needed lots of help.

Suddenly a message came over the radio. It called out, "S. O. S.—Save Our Ship!" Mr. Pennyfeather listened carefully. A big ship carrying hundreds of people was lost in the fog and needed Willie's light to find its way into the harbor.

"They need you, Willie!" Mr. Pennyfeather said. "You must turn on your light now!" He worked and worked and finally Willie's light went on. It was dim at first but it grew brighter.

The big ship sent out another S. O. S. Mr. Pennyfeather blinked Willie's light over and over. "We'll save 'em, Willie! We can do it!" he said.

They blinked and blinked and at last another message came over the radio. "We see your light. We know where we are now. Thank you, Willie!" it said. Willie's blinking light had saved the big ship and the hundreds of people it was carrying.

But Mr. Pennyfeather had blinked so hard that Willie's light burned itself out. It would never go on again.

The next morning a shiny green truck drove up to the lighthouse. Four men from Washington stepped out. From the truck they unloaded buckets of paint, a new light, and a big new rescue boat. Then they all went to work.

At the end of the day Willie looked like a young, important lighthouse. The biggest man from Washington said to Mr. Pennyfeather, "I guess we need you and Willie after all!"

Mr. Pennyfeather was proud. He knew Willie was proud, too.

That night Willie's new light looked out over the big blue ocean and seemed to be shouting to all the ships, *"Don't worry! You'll never get lost now!"*

Timothy Buys a Pet

By Gertrude Blumenthal

Ever since he was very little, Timothy had wanted a puppy dog. Always his daddy and mother said, "When you are older, we will buy you one." Now Timothy was five, old enough, he thought, to have a puppy.

"Yes," his mother and daddy agreed. "We'll get Timothy his puppy."

So, one fine Saturday afternoon, they all went to the pet shop to choose a dog.

The window in the pet shop was divided into two parts. Six puppies were rolling about in shredded paper in one half, and kittens were playing in the other. When Timothy's father tapped on the glass, all the dogs began to bark and jump about. The kittens stopped playing just long enough to look at them, and then went right back to rolling over each other.

On an upper level, in the same window, was a large cage full of white bunnies. But they just sat looking out at Timothy, their pink eyes very bright.

"Let's go in," said Mother. "I'm sure there are talking parrots, too."

Inside it was warm and noisy, in a nice kind of way. Dogs barked. Birds whistled and twittered. Cats made scratchy sounds with their claws. There were fishes swimming about in large bowls. There were baby alligators and turtles over in the far corner.

Mr. Dingle who owned the shop was a little man, very fat and very jolly. He had rosy red cheeks and he wore glasses. Most of the time the glasses were pushed up above his forehead. When they were where they should be, Mr. Dingle didn't look through them, he looked over them.

Now he was looking over them as he bent down to talk to Timothy.

"So you want a puppy, do you? Any special kind of a puppy? We have fat ones and skinny ones and little ones and long ones. But if you'd rather have a monkey, we have some fine specimens back there."

They walked way back into the shop, and sure enough, over in a corner in a big cage, were four of the sweetest monkeys Timothy had ever seen.

They were playing tag, racing each other all over the cage. The littlest one stopped playing long enough to swing back and forth on his skinny tail. While he was hanging upside down, he noticed Timothy. He took a flying leap and landed at the bottom of the cage, right in front of him. Then he put his paw between the bars and shook hands with Timothy. When the other monkeys saw what was happening, they came hurrying over too, chattering away in a funny jibber-jabber.

His father said, "They're trying to be your friends, too. How about shaking hands all around?"

Timothy tried to shake hands with all the monkeys, but the littlest one would not let go. He scolded the monkeys, and he scolded Timothy. He set up such a noise, Mr. Dingle came to see what was going on.

"Tsk, tsk," he said. "They are a noisy lot. They like little boys. You're the first one in today, and they want to show off. What do you think of my babies?"

"I like them." Timothy couldn't pull his hand away from the littlest monkey. "They must be fun. Daddy, what do you say we buy a monkey instead of a dog?"

Mr. Dingle interrupted. "You wouldn't be sorry. They are the gentlest, cleanest, lovingest things in the world. Easy to raise, if you watch their diet. Just sold one yesterday to a man down the street."

But Timothy's mother would have none of it. "I don't mind a puppy. He's always underfoot, that's true. But a monkey—why you'd never know where to look for him."

"Most likely he'd be swinging from the curtain rods or hanging on the picture frames," said Father.

"But, Daddy, they're so cute," Timothy argued. "I'd watch him every minute to be sure he didn't get into things. Mother, let's buy a monkey. You won't be sorry."

"You're all the monkey I want," his mother said. "We came to buy a puppy. If you've changed your mind, that's all right. We can do without a puppy. We have for so long, it won't matter."

Timothy was on the point of tears. He wanted a monkey awfully bad.

But the monkeys themselves settled the problem. Suddenly one of them picked up the water dish from the bottom of the cage and flung it right at Timothy. He was only playing, but the water came as such a wet, cold surprise, Timothy and his parents couldn't say a word. They got splashed all over. Mr. Dingle burst out laughing. "The little scoundrel," he said, "first time he ever did that—last time, too!"

He went over, opened the cage, and reached in for the monkey. He scampered away, the others after him, high up into the cage where Mr. Dingle couldn't reach. There they sat, scolding.

Mr. Dingle closed the cage. "I'll give him his just desserts later," he said. "Now, Timothy, did you say you wanted a dog?"

Brushing the water from their clothes, Timothy and

his mother and daddy followed Mr. Dingle out to the kennels.

The dogs leaped about in their cages, yipping and barking, trying to get out. When they saw Timothy and all the other people, they tried to get at them, and the noise they made was terrific.

"How do you stand it?" asked Mrs. Brown. "It would drive me frantic."

"Oh, you get used to it, just as you do to a baby crying. The little fellows are lonesome. After all, dogs were meant to be with people, not behind fences. Most of the time, though, they are pretty quiet."

While they were talking, Timothy walked up and down trying to decide which dog he'd like best. The little ones were so cute, he couldn't see how anyone could choose from among them.

There were Airedales, collies, bull terriers. There were French bulls and dachshunds. There were wire-haired terriers and Scotties. There were setters, spaniels, and hounds. There was a great Dane and a Russian wolfhound and a Saint Bernard. The great Dane was only six weeks old, but it looked like a grown dog instead of a puppy. And the same thing was true of the Saint Bernard.

Of course Timothy couldn't tell them apart. Neither could his daddy or his mother. Mr. Dingle walked up and down and pointed out the different breeds.

"I'll tell you what," he said. "If you want a good out-of-door kind of dog, get a collie. He's playful and he loves to romp about. If you want a smaller type of dog, more for staying indoors, get a Sealyham. He's such a funny dog. I mean he likes to clown and do tricks. Or you might get a dachshund. They're affectionate dogs and very loyal. I wouldn't choose any of the big breeds, because they need lots of room to grow in—and lots of exercise while they are growing."

Mrs. Brown liked a dachshund. Mr. Brown thought a spaniel was fine. But Timothy couldn't decide. He liked them all.

"I'll tell you what," Mr. Dingle suggested. "Pick out six dogs of different breeds and I'll put them in a separate kennel. Then you can choose one out of six instead of one out of twenty-six."

That was a good idea, but even one from six was hard. They had a dachshund, a spaniel, a fox terrier, a Scotty, a French poodle, and a Boston bull.

Timothy studied them all very carefully. Somehow he liked the dachshund the least. So Mr. Dingle put the little brown dog back with his sisters and brothers. Now they had five.

Mrs. Brown didn't like poodles. "I think a French poodle is silly. Not when it's little, but when it gets bigger. Must they shave its neck and legs the way they do, Mr. Dingle? I think they look silly."

Timothy remembered seeing just such a dog once, and he didn't like him. So they put the poodle back in its cage. Now they had four.

Mr. Brown looked them over carefully. The dogs were all playful, all but the spaniel. He lay there with his head between his paws, looking up at them with sad, brown eyes.

"Why does he look so sad?" Timothy asked. "He makes me want to cry."

"He's not sad," said Mr. Dingle. "He's just not in the mood."

"But he ought to be excited like the rest. After all, he might get a new master," said Timothy.

"He's a sweet fellow," said Mrs. Brown, "but I don't like moody dogs. Suppose we put him back?"

So now they had three.

The fox terrier was white all over, with big brown spots on his back. The Scotty was inky black and the Boston bull was black, too, with a big white ring around one eye.

Mr. Dingle thought the Scotty would be the best. But Mrs. Brown wondered about a dog with long hair. "After all, Timothy, he might shed all over the place. I don't especially like the idea of chasing him off chairs and rugs because of the hair." So now there were two.

Now they really had a hard time, because both dogs were so cute. And both dogs sat up on their hind legs and begged.

"Can't we have both?" Timothy begged. "I could take care of two as easy as one."

Mrs. Brown shook her head. "One, Timothy. One, till we are sure we like a dog around the house."

"Yes," said Mr. Brown. "One will be quite a handful. You had better decide on one."

"But, Daddy, they're both so cute. I don't know which to take."

Mr. Dingle said, "Shut your eyes and choose."

Mrs. Brown said, "Think which one would play nicely with your friends, too."

And while Timothy stood there, trying to decide, the little Boston bull winked at him, out of the eye with the white ring around it.

Timothy was so excited he could hardly speak.

"Daddy, Mother, did you see? He winked at me. Look." They all looked hard, and sure enough, right out of the eye with the big white ring, came a wink.

That settled it. Any dog that could do that, was just the right dog for a boy. So Timothy chose the Boston bull puppy.

Everyone was quite happy about it. Mr. Brown said he really hoped Timothy would choose him. And Mrs. Brown said she had her eye on him all the time. And Mr. Dingle—well, he wouldn't say yes and he wouldn't say no. After all, he wanted to find good homes for all his dogs.

They bought a little bed for the puppy. They bought a harness and a leash. They bought a rubber bone for the dog to play with. And they bought puppy food. They bought a book that told them all about how to raise a dog.

"If you have any questions, Timothy," said Mr. Dingle, "just stop by and let me help you out."

Timothy was so excited about his dog, he didn't hear a word anyone said. He held the puppy tight in his arms. And the puppy reached up, every now and then, and licked Timothy's face.

Mr. Brown carried all the belongings out to the car. Then they all got settled in the front seat. Mr. Brown at the wheel. Timothy and the dog in the middle.

And Mrs. Brown on the outside.

"Well, here we are," said Mr. Brown. "All snug as a bug in a rug."

Mrs. Brown said, "Home, James."

And Timothy said, "Guess what I'm going to name him? Winkie. He winked at me, that's why I picked him. That's what I'll call him, Winkie."

So that was how Timothy chose his dog. And that's why his dog was called Winkie.

Petunia

By Alice Sankey

Way down south where the winters are sunny there lived a poor little pelican named Petunia. Most of Petunia's neighbors seemed to have enough money to buy anything they wanted. Petunia was different. She did not have enough money to buy anything at all.

Petunia's next-door neighbor was a proud, pink flamingo. He was called Flim-Flam.

Petunia once asked, "Why do they call the flamingo Flim-Flam?"

"You will find out," a stork told her. "If ever you have anything the flamingo wants for himself, the first thing he will do will be to play some trick to get it."

"No flim-flamming flamingo will get anything that belongs to *me*," said Petunia.

The little pelican just had to figure out some way to make a living. She hung up a sign:

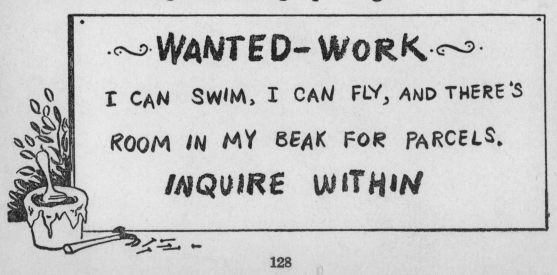

She waited all day for someone to offer her work. Many would stop to read the sign and then go next door.

"There's something wrong with that sign," said Petunia.

She went out to read it. It looked all right until she came to the last line. Instead of saying INQUIRE WITHIN it read INQUIRE NEXT DOOR.

"Well, for land's sake," said Petunia. "I do believe I am being flim-flammed by the flamingo!"

She hurried next door as fast as she could waddle. She found the flamingo saying to a group of callers, "I have all the jobs listed and everything will be done."

He looked up, and there was Petunia.

"What do you mean by changing my sign and taking all my customers away?" asked Petunia angrily.

The flamingo could not think of a thing to say for a moment. Then he bowed. "I was just trying to be a good neighbor," he said.

"Good neighbors do not take customers away," said Petunia.

"Tut-tut! How do you know I took them away? I thought there were more customers than one pelican could take care of, so I made a list of them. We can be partners."

"But I don't *want* to be a partner," said Petunia.

"Tut-tut! How do you know you don't want to be a

partner? I have a list of jobs to be done. Have you?"

"Well, no," said Petunia. "But—"

"Tut-tut! There is work to be done. We must not waste time talking. I will pay you ten cents an hour, with time and a half for overtime. That's fair, isn't it?"

"But—but—" sputtered Petunia.

"Tut-tut!" said the flamingo. "Someone wants a message delivered across the lake. I'll tell you what I'm going to do. I find that my legs are too long for fast swimming. I'm going to let you do that job. Hurry!"

Before Petunia could think of another thing to say, she found herself halfway across the lake.

Petunia was a very fast swimmer. She came back all out of breath. Flim-Flam handed her some golf clubs.

"Tut-tut!" said the flamingo. "My legs are so long that I walk too fast for the golfers. I'm going to let *you* caddy. The golfer is waiting."

Petunia carried the golf clubs in her beak as best she could, leaving the ends sticking out so that the golfer could pick out the ones he wanted. An hour later she came back. The little pelican was beginning to get tired.

"Tut-tut!" said the flamingo. "There's no time for resting. A customer wants someone to fly over the swamp to deliver a kitten to a friend. But my wing feathers are too short for fast flying. Here is what

I'm going to do. I'm going to let *you* deliver the kitten."

Petunia carried the kitten in her beak and soared out over the swamp. The little pelican was a very good flyer. She could dip and turn and swirl to land in the exact spot where she wanted to go. In almost no time at all she was back again. She was all out of breath. The flamingo met her with some packages.

"There is a birthday party at the hotel. I'll tell you what I'm going to do. I have no pouch in my beak, so I'm going to let *you* deliver the birthday presents," said Flim-Flam.

Petunia was all worn out when she returned. She knew she had worked hard, and she was ready to collect her pay. When she got back, she found the flamingo counting out the money in two piles. A big pile and a little one.

"Four jobs. We had a very good day," said the flamingo.

"I did all four of the jobs," said Petunia.

"Tut-tut!" said the flamingo. "Don't bother me when I'm busy counting."

He pointed to the smallest pile.

"That is your share," he said.

Petunia reached for it, but before she could take it, Flim-Flam stopped her.

"Tut-tut! I forgot to take ten cents for my notebook," said Flim-Flam. He took ten cents from Petunia's pile.

"And ten cents for the wear and tear on my path," said Flim-Flam. He took another ten cents from Petunia's pile.

"And ten cents for staying here all day.

"And ten cents for talking to the people.

"And ten cents for keeping track of the jobs.

"And ten cents—"

"Just a minute!" yelled Petunia. She picked up the five cents—all that was left of her pile. She was so angry she could not talk, but she knew if she waited one minute longer, the flamingo would think of a way to get her last five cents.

She was so tired that she did not stay to argue.

"Expenses are always high when you start a new business," Flim-Flam called after her.

The next morning Petunia Pelican was still angry. The more she thought about doing all that work for five cents, the angrier she became.

The stork stopped to see her soon after breakfast.

"The whole town is talking about the way you got flim-flammed by the flamingo," the stork told her.

"Today I shall teach him a lesson," said Petunia.

"How?" asked the stork.

"I am thinking about it," said Petunia.

She saw Mr. Penguin, the owner of the big hotel, going next door. She followed him. He began to talk to Flim-Flam.

"I have read the sign, *I can swim, I can fly, and there's room in my beak for parcels*. I am willing to hire this worker full time and pay him a lot of money. Do you want the job?" he asked.

Before Flim-Flam could answer, Petunia spoke up.

"Mr. Penguin, before you hire anyone, I think you should try him out to see if he can do the work. I am willing to take a test."

"Tut-tut! We are partners," said Flim-Flam.

"Oh, no. That was yesterday," said Petunia.

"You have a good idea," said Mr. Penguin, the hotel man. "Who would like to try first?"

"Tut-tut!" said Flim-Flam. "I talked to you first. I deserve to try first."

"Very well," said Petunia.

She pretended to go home, but she wanted to see what Flim-Flam was going to do. The flamingo went with Mr. Penguin to the hotel and Petunia followed.

The first errand the flamingo had to do was to swim across the lake. He tried to get a duck to go for him.

"Oh, no," said the duck. "Not after the way you flim-flammed Petunia."

The flamingo was afraid to try it himself, so he left the errand undone.

His second task was to deliver some messages by air. He tried to get a pigeon to do it for him.

"Oh, no," said the pigeon. "Not after the way you flim-flammed Petunia."

So the messages were not delivered.

His next errand was to carry packages from a store to the guests in the hotel. He tried to get an ostrich to help him.

"Oh, no," said the ostrich. "Not after the way you flim-flammed Petunia."

So the packages were not delivered.

The next job was to wait on table. He asked the stork to do it for him.

"Oh, no," said the stork. "Not after the way you flim-flammed Petunia."

Flim-Flam could not hold the tray in his curved beak, and he broke two dozen dishes.

Mr. Penguin, the hotel man, was angry.

"Go away, and don't come back," he shouted at Flim-Flam.

Petunia stepped forward.

"I can swim, I can fly, and there's room in my beak for parcels," said Petunia.

"You're hired," said Mr. Penguin. "I was afraid the flamingo was trying to flim-flam me into thinking he would work, and I guess I was right."

Petunia thanked Mr. Penguin for hiring her, then she turned to Flim-Flam.

"I'll tell you what I'm going to do," she said. "I will be busy from now on, so I'm going to let you go home and take down the sign."

Everybody laughed but Flim-Flam, the flamingo. He was feeling *very* foolish.

PELICAN AIR EXPRESS

Pom Pom

By Virginia Cunningham

Pom Pom the poodle was a downtown dog. He lived in Mamzelle Mimi's French Hat Shop on the Boulevard.

The hats in Mamzelle Mimi's French Hat Shop were fancy indeed. They had feathers, ribbons, and roses.

But there wasn't a hat in the shop that was any fancier than Pom Pom himself.

Pom Pom's hair was the blackest, the curliest, the woolliest hair any poodle ever had. If Mamzelle had let it alone, Pom Pom would have been just woolly black curls all over.

But Mamzelle Mimi said, "My hats are in style. My dog must be in style, too. But yes!"

And so she had Pom Pom's black woolly curls clipped and plucked in the latest French fashion.

He had one little round pompon of curls on top of his head. And he had another round little pompon on the end of his tail. Across his shoulders was a mane as thick as a lion's. But his neck was clipped smooth so that he could show off his silver collar.

"Oo-la-la," said Mamzelle Mimi when she saw Pom Pom's new hairdo. "What style! I shall design a pompon hat to match you."

And so she did.

At first Pom Pom felt very silly. And he felt a little chilly, too. But the ladies who came to the hat shop made such a fuss over him that he soon began to feel very pleased with himself. And besides, that pompon on the end of his tail was very good for switching flies.

Pom Pom liked to sit on his stool by the window and look out between the hats at the people going by on the Boulevard. It was his own special stool with a yellow silk cushion on it.

The people liked to look at Pom Pom, too. Quite often the ladies came inside the shop to shake hands with Pom Pom or to pat his curly head.

Then Mamzelle Mimi would sell them a pompon hat quickly—before they had time to remember why they had come in.

One rainy afternoon there were no customers. Mamzelle Mimi went back to her little kitchenette behind the shop to fix a cup of tea.

Pom Pom sat on his cushion and watched the rain.

All at once he heard a noise at the door.

Scritch, scratch. Meow!

It was a cat. A cat was meowing at Pom Pom's own door!

"Yap-yap," barked Pom Pom, jumping up angrily. "Yap-yap. Woof. Gr-rr-rr!"

Through the glass he saw a wet black cat.

"Meow," said the cat. "Mee-ow!"

"Yap, yap!" barked Pom Pom.

Mamzelle Mimi came rushing out into the shop.

She saw the little wet black head peeking at her through the glass.

"Oh, you poor little kitty-cat," she cried.

There was a certain tone in her voice that told Pom Pom Mamzelle was *not* going to shoo the cat away.

And she didn't. She rushed right over to the door, opened it, and picked up the little cat.

Mamzelle began rubbing the cat dry with a soft towel. "Purr-rr," sang the cat happily.

The cat purred even louder when Mamzelle Mimi fixed her a dish of warm milk. She lapped up every bit with her little pink tongue.

Pom Pom could hardly believe his eyes. A cat right in his own house! How could a self-respecting dog stand for that? Pom Pom turned his back on Mamzelle and sulked. But he was so curious that he had to turn around again.

"Good dog, Pom Pom," said Mamzelle. "You are a good dog to tell me to come and get the cat. If you hadn't barked, I would never have known she was there."

Pom Pom was too surprised even to say yap.

Then Mamzelle put on her overshoes and her raincoat and took her big red umbrella.

"I shall go to the store," she said. "I shall get some meat for my good Pom Pom and his little cat friend."

And off she went.

Pom Pom glared fiercely at the cat.

And the cat glared back at Pom Pom.

"Gr-rr," said Pom Pom, meaning, "I won't have a cat in *my* house."

"Hiss-ss," said the little cat. "I'll stay in this house if I please."

Pom Pom crouched ready to spring, and zoom! the cat was off across the shop like a furry black cannon ball.

At the other end of the shop was a hat tree. It had a hat on every branch.

The cat saw the hat tree right away. It looked just like any other tree to her, and the hats looked like big blossoms—or maybe apples. She knew that a tree was a good place to be when a dog was chasing her.

So she took a flying leap for it.

But instead of standing still, as trees had always done before, this tree wobbled wildly in the air.

BANG! It crashed to the floor.

The cat leaped to the counter.

Hats flew every which way.

A red straw bonnet trimmed

with butterflies landed right on Pom Pom's head.

"Yap-yap," yelled poor Pom Pom, and he began clawing at the horrible thing that covered his eyes.

Rip! Rip!

And he tore off the top of the hat.

But the brim still hung around his neck like a Christmas holly wreath. And a butterfly bobbed over each ear.

Pom Pom looked very silly, but he didn't know it so he didn't care.

At least now he could see where he was going. And he could chase that cat.

"Gr-r-r," growled Pom Pom, trying to sound very fierce. He'd teach that cat to mind her own business and stay out of his house!

Just then Mamzelle Mimi came back.

She stood outside the door shaking the raindrops off her umbrella. Then she opened the door and came in. She took one look at the hat shop. And she took one look at Pom Pom. And she began to scream.

"Ee-ee! Bad dog! Bad dog! My hat! My beautiful hat! Ruined. Ruined."

Pom Pom did not care about the hat. All he wanted was to *get that cat!*

But where was the cat?

Pom Pom looked all over the shop. There were hats

on the floor. Hats on the chairs. Hats on the tables and counter. Hats in every corner.

But no cat.

Pom Pom did not see two furry little black ears and two bright eyes peeking over the rim of a green hat upside down on the counter.

The little cat was safe inside that green hat and she meant to stay there.

All of a sudden Pom Pom noticed the green hat. He cocked his head on one side and looked at it carefully.

Was he seeing things?

Or had that green hat really moved?

The green hat was as still as still.

Pom Pom cocked his head on the other side.

No, the green hat did not move.

So Pom Pom began to look for the cat somewhere else.

He looked behind every table.

He looked under every chair.

He looked in every corner.

No cat.

Then Pom Pom started his search all over again.

He looked in every corner.

He looked under every chair.

He even looked in the mirror.

No cat.

Mamzelle Mimi was so upset about the hats that

she forgot all about the little black cat.

She picked up the hats one by one and put them back on the hat tree.

Pom Pom sat down in the middle of the floor. He had a very puzzled look on his face.

Everything was so quiet that by and by the little cat peeked out again over the rim of the hat.

And just then a mouse came creeping out from behind the counter.

The cat jumped to get the mouse.

And Pom Pom jumped to get the cat.

The mouse jumped to get back to its hole.

And Mamzelle jumped up on the counter.

"Ee-ee-ee!" screamed Mamzelle. "A mouse! Ee-ee-ee!"

She screamed so loudly that Pom Pom skidded to a

stop. He forgot all about chasing the cat. He just stood still in the middle of the room and stared at Mamzelle. What was the matter with her?

The cat was so frightened by the screams that she stopped chasing the mouse and hid under a chair.

The mouse scooted down its hole—quick!

When Mamzelle was sure that the mouse was gone she stopped screaming and climbed from the counter. The cat peeked out from under the chair ruffle, but Pom Pom just sat and stared at Mamzelle Mimi.

"Oo-la-la!" Mamzelle gasped. "What excitement!"

She sat down on a chair and fanned herself with a hat until she got her breath.

"Good dog, Pom Pom!" she said at last. "You are a good dog to chase the mouse. Now I know how you knocked down my hats. You were chasing the mouse, of course. So I forgive you. I forgive your little cat friend, too. She may live here with us always. Come, I will fix you both some supper."

Pom Pom looked at the cat.

The cat looked at Pom Pom. Very slowly she winked one eye.

Pom Pom wagged his tail.

Then side by side they followed Mamzelle into the kitchenette.

SUSAN and the RAIN

By Madye Lee Chastain

Susan Amantha Cottonwood
   Was a little girl
     who was always good——
When the sun shone.
But when the clouds piled up in the sky
And began to rain—she would *cry!*
   And *cry* and *moan!*
Susan Amantha hated the rain.
She would press her nose to the windowpane
   And complain,
     And complain,
       And complain!
"There's *nothing* to do if I can't play outside——
If the sun was out, I'd take my doll for a ride,
I'd bounce my ball, I'd swing on the gate;
I'd go round the block on one roller skate!
But there's nothing to do in the whole wide world—
   When it rains!"

Now, one summer she went to the country
  To visit her grandpapa,
And her uncles and aunts and cousins,
  And her grandmamma.
She played in the barn on the piles of hay——
She played in the meadow the livelong day.
The sun shone bright and Susan was gay!
But one day——
It *rained!*
And Susan *complained!*

Her grandpapa was amazed to hear
So many complaints and he said, "I fear
You don't know why we have the rain
Or you *wouldn't* complain!
We have the rain to water the crops,
To make fine lettuce and big beet tops.
It makes the corn tall—row on row,
And the apples juicy, and the blackberries grow.
It fills the rivers and streams and lakes.
It softens the soil the gardener rakes.
It washes the dust from all the leaves
And makes a song as it drips from the eaves.
Why, nothing would grow on our very own farm—
If it didn't *rain*.
Susan—*Don't* complain!"
Susan Amantha Cottonwood
Told Grandpapa that she understood—
But just the same
   It wasn't much fun
      When there was no sun!

Susan went home and though she *tried,*
Nevertheless, when it rained, she cried.
Until——
One day the postman rang the bell.
Mother opened the door and said, "Well, well!
Here's a package for Susan from Grandpapa."
When Susan got the strings untied
And opened the box, she found inside,
A bright red umbrella, shiny black boots,
And a red plaid raincoat
With a rainhat to suit!
Well, the next time it rained
Did Susan *complain?*
NO!

She put on her boots
And her raincoat and hat
And she took her umbrella and went spitty-spat
Out in the rain——and in all the puddles!
Rain thumped her umbrella
Rain spattered her coat;
Each boot was as wet as a shiny black boat.
She splashed and she sploshed,
As happy as could be, and she said——
"Why the rain *is* fun,
And it's raining *just* for *me!*"

149

By Madye Lee Chastain

Emmaline Eliza Porter Brown was a little girl who lived in a small town in the big state of Texas about the time your grandmother was a little girl. She thought life was very fine indeed. She lived with her mother and her father and her grandmamma and grandpapa.

Mother had a wonderful hat trimmed with two ostrich plumes, three red roses and a bird's nest with a bird in it.

Father had a very special mustache cup that kept his beautiful black mustache dry when he drank his morning coffee.

Grandmamma wore three taffeta petticoats—a black one, a red one, and a plaid one—and they swished when she walked.

Grandpapa smoked a long pipe and the bowl was shaped like a dog's head.

Emmaline Eliza Porter Brown had a doll house with six rooms.

She had a doll carriage, too. It had a pink and green top with fringe all around.

And she had a beautiful china doll named Miranda Sue. This doll had a little trunk of its own filled with dresses and shoes and hats, and a tiny handbag with a penny in it.

They all lived together in a very large house.

Behind the house there was a stable. In one side of this stable there was a shiny black surrey, and in the other side there was a shiny black horse, named Nellie.

Now Emmaline Eliza Porter Brown loved her doll house and her doll carriage and her doll, but most of all she loved the shiny black horse. She would swing on the stable door and watch Nellie eating hay and oats. She would hang over the fence and watch Nellie eating grass in the back lot.

The most exciting days were Sundays when father hitched Nellie to the shiny black surrey and took the family for a drive in the country.

"What a fine day for a drive," Grandpapa would say.

"How nice the air is," Grandmamma would say.

"How fresh everything looks," Mother would say.

"A fine day *indeed*!" Father would say.

"How I wish I could drive Nellie!" Emmaline would think to herself. *Think,* mind you, she didn't actually say it! Because one day she *had* said it—right out loud! *"Oh, I wish I could drive Nellie!"* she had said. Everyone just *looked* at her!

"Sakes, no!" said Grandmamma.

"Lands, no!" said Grandpapa.

"Oh, dear, no!" said Mother.

"No, *indeed!*" said Father.

Those were a great many "No's" all at once and Emmaline didn't say another word all the way home —but she watched. She always watched how Father held the reins and said "Gee up" and "Whoa." And all the while she thought to herself, "I could drive Nellie!" Because, you see, although Grandmamma and Grandpapa and Mother and Father thought Emmaline was a very *little* girl, Emmaline thought she was a very *big* girl. And she was quite sure she could drive a horse and surrey.

Now one day Emmaline Eliza Porter Brown and her mother and father and grandmamma and grandpapa drove into town to do some shopping. They stopped in front of Mr. McMullan's Dry Goods Store. Mother went in to buy some black silk mitts. And Grandmamma went in to buy some tatting thread. Father walked down the street to the bank. That left Grandpapa and Emmaline sitting in the surrey.

Just then Grandpapa remembered he had no tobacco for his pipe.

"I'll be back in two minutes," said Grandpapa, hurrying off down the street to Mr. Dill's Tobacco Shop.

That left Emmaline Eliza Porter Brown all alone in the surrey. All alone with Nellie. Now she didn't really mean to pick up the reins—she just wanted to see how they felt in her hands. And she didn't really intend to

say "Gee up"—at least not very loud. But Nellie heard her. She picked up her ears, shook her head and started off down the street. Emmaline was so surprised she couldn't say a word at first. When she finally found her tongue, she was so scared she hollered "Gee up" when she really meant to holler "Whoa!" Of course when Nellie heard "Gee up" she just trotted that much faster. Emmaline was so frightened, she just held on very tight and tried to keep from bouncing too much.

Nellie trotted smartly past the shoemaker's and the barber shop and the bank. She trotted past Mr. Dill's Tobacco Shop and Miss Abigail's Confectionery Shop.

And because Emmaline kept shouting "Gee up!" when she really meant "Whoa!" Nellie trotted still faster past Dooley's Livery Stable, Miss Seller's Bookstore and the Court House.

By the time they reached the road that ran beside the railroad tracks, Nellie was trotting very fast indeed. But that wasn't half as fast as she trotted when

she saw the passenger train coming down the tracks.

The engineer leaned out of his window and waved, for he thought Nellie wanted to race. Nellie began to run faster because she thought the engineer wanted to race.

The engineer tooted his whistle. Then Nellie really ran! So fast that Emmaline thought the pink and blue flowers by the side of the road looked like a colored ribbon rushing by. Nellie wasn't running away—she was just having fun. The engineer was having fun, too —and kept tooting his whistle. But Emmaline wasn't having fun. She just held tight to the reins and kept shouting "Gee up" when she really meant "Whoa!" of course.

Just when Emmaline thought she would surely bounce out of the surrey, the engineer gave a final toot on the whistle and waved his hand, for here the tracks turned away toward the next town.

When Nellie saw the train disappearing she knew the race was over so she stopped running. In fact, she stopped still and began nibbling the grass at the side of the road. Emmaline was so shaken up from all the bouncing that it was a minute before she heard her name being called and the sound of another horse coming up the road behind her.

It was Father in Mr. McMullan's delivery wagon. Emmaline Eliza Porter Brown was very glad to see Father. Father was very glad to see her, too. In fact, he was so glad to see that she was safe, he didn't scold her for trying to drive Nellie.

Emmaline didn't really need scolding for she had learned quite well that she wasn't big enough to drive a horse and surrey.

When they drove home that afternoon, Grandpapa said, "My, it was a fine day for a drive to town."

"And the air was very nice," said Grandmamma.

"Everything looked so fresh," said Mother.

"Oh, yes, it was a fine day, indeed," said Emmaline Eliza Porter Brown in a very small voice.

And do you know what Nellie did?

SHE LAUGHED!

TATTERS

Tatters was Bobby's funny little fuzzy dog that always wanted to hide.

Tatters especially wanted to hide from Bobby when there was work to do, such as picking up his toy bone, and his rubber mouse, and his ting-a-ling ball, and when he was supposed to eat every last crumb of his puppy biscuit.

He could wriggle his fuzzy little self into the strangest places! He would climb into a boot or slip into the clothespin bag.

He could scrooch under a pillow, sometimes in a chair, sometimes in a bed, or perhaps even in the doll carriage.

"Tatters! Tatters!" Bobby would call.

Tatters would be as quiet as a mouse, but Bobby would always find him.

One day Tatters found a really good hiding place—the broom closet!

He hid way back in a corner, and when he tried to peek he found the door was shut!

Bobby called and called, but poor Tatters couldn't get out.

Tatters sat and wondered what he could do to help Bobby find him, when suddenly the closet door opened, Bobby's mother reached in, and SPLASH! Poor Tatters found himself in a pail of soapy water!

Then he was lifted out of the pail and swished around in a circle on the floor before he could catch his breath.

Bobby was right there. He heard his mother scream and saw her jump onto the table.

"Oh-h-h-h-h! That mop sneezed!" she said.

Bobby laughed and laughed. He knew it was Tatters, and his mother had been fooled.

Do you think Tatters tries to hide any more?

No, indeed.

He sits in the middle of the room!

PieFace

By Velma Doreith

The gate of the first house on Cherry Lane had a big sign:

BEWARE OF THE DOG

That was where King, the brown-and-white collie lived.

King was such a big dog, with such a loud bark that most strangers were quite ready to beware of him, even without the sign.

But the neighbors often saw King playing with Tim, his owner. The boy and the dog rolled and tumbled and pretended to fight. But King never left a scratch or a tooth mark on Tim's hand.

So none of the neighbors paid any attention to the sign.

The gate of the second house had a medium-sized sign:

That was where Muggsy, the bulldog, lived. Any strangers who came near Muggsy's yard took one look at his ugly face, listened to his vicious growl, and did not come any closer.

But when no strangers were around, Muggsy let three-year-old Tommy sit on his back without complaining.

Or Tommy would dress him up in Father's old clothes, or use him for a pillow.

Muggsy's temper was not as ugly as his face.

The gate of the third house had no sign. And no dog lived in the house. But Penny and Denny, the red-headed twins who lived there, wanted a dog very much. They had written their grandmother a letter and told her so.

Grandmother had written Penny and Denny a letter saying she would send them a dog for their birthday.

And *today* was their birthday.

"Maybe she'll send us a police dog," said Denny. "Police dogs are swell watch dogs."

"Maybe she'll send us a great Dane," said Penny. "They're just about the biggest dogs in the world!"

"Or a bloodhound," said Denny. "Then we can be detectives!"

"Anyhow," said Penny, "we can have a sign on our gate. Just like Tim and Tommy."

Just then an express truck came up the street. It stopped right in front of the house.

The driver called out, "Package for Penny and Denny Marsh! Where do you want it?"

"Right here," said Denny.

The man carried the crate up on the porch. "Here, I'll help you open it," he said.

"Be careful," warned Penny. "It's our dog!"

"That's what the sign says," agreed the man. "But looks pretty small for a dog. Maybe they just sent the fleas and forgot the dog."

But it *was* a dog. Out he jumped—still barking. But he was so little!

"Call *that* a dog?" said the express man.

"Sure!" said Denny, and added, "he'll grow."

"Not that kind!" said the man. "Those dogs don't get any bigger. Well, sign here for it."

"We'd better take it in and feed it," said Denny. "It sure won't grow if it doesn't eat. Come on, pooch!" The little dog pricked up his ears and trotted into the house.

"Look!" said Denny. "He doesn't even *walk* like a dog. He trots like a pony."

"And his ears!" said Penny. "They look like donkey's ears."

While Penny and Denny rummaged in the icebox for something to feed him, the little dog went snooping around the kitchen.

"Shall we give him this meat?" asked Denny.

"No," said Penny. "That's for supper."

"Well, we can give him some milk, anyhow. There's plenty of that," said Denny.

"Here, pooch!" began Denny. And then he stopped, "Hey! What are you doing up on that table?"

"He's eating my pie! My own piece of butterscotch pie that I saved for supper!"

The little dog looked up. There was butterscotch pie on his nose. There was butterscotch pie on his whiskers. And there was a big blob of meringue over his left eyebrow.

"Oh," said Denny. "You pie face, you!"

The little dog reached out his long pink tongue and began licking the butterscotch off his nose and off his whiskers—but he couldn't quite reach the meringue on his left eyebrow.

"Here, I'll help you wash your face," said Penny, and she got a damp cloth. "You little pie face!" she scolded.

"Pie Face!" said Denny. "That's a good name for a pie-eating, sissy dog! Pie Face!"

The little dog knew he was being scolded. He put back his ears and rolled his eyes.

Just then Mother came home from the store. "Good heavens!" she said. "What's that?"

"Why, that's our dog," said Penny.

"But Grandmother said she was sending you a Cairn terrier—a pedigreed dog—registered with the American Kennel Club. Is that what this is? Let me read that letter again.

"'. . . Cairn terrier . . . almost a year old . . . nice house dog . . . won't grow any bigger . . . will send registration certificate later . . .'

"Registration certificate means he's a thoroughbred dog," Mother explained, interrupting herself, "and he's listed in the books of the American Kennel Club. At least he's a *good* dog, even if he isn't a very big one."

"Let's put up a 'beware of the dog' sign now," said Penny to her brother.

"Don't be silly," said Denny. "No one bewares of such a little dog."

"We could have just a very *small* sign," pleaded Penny. "Someone might beware just a little."

"Not even a small sign," said Denny firmly. "No one would beware of Pie Face at all. He's a sissy. Who ever heard of a dog that eats butterscotch pie?"

"You eat butterscotch pie," argued Penny. "And of course *you* aren't a sissy."

"With me it's different," said Denny. "Dogs should eat bones and raw meat and dog biscuits."

"And boys should eat spinach and carrots and oatmeal," Penny teased.

"Oh, phooey!" said Denny. "Why couldn't Grandmother have sent us a man-sized dog like King, the collie? Or a pooch with a vicious-looking mug like Muggsy?"

"I'm sure Pie Face won't ever look like Muggsy," said Penny. "And it's a good thing! But I do wish he'd get bigger."

"Not a chance!" said Denny. "Grandmother's letter said he wouldn't. He'll always be a good-for-nothing little sissy."

Pie Face seemed to know they were talking about him. He jumped onto Denny's lap, put his front feet on Denny's shoulder, and stretched up to his full height of eighteen inches.

Penny laughed. "See, Denny," she said. "He's trying to *look* big."

"Humph!" humphed Denny, unimpressed.

"And anyway," Penny went on, reaching over and scratching Pie Face behind the ear, "maybe he isn't completely good-for-nothing. *Some* small dogs catch rats."

Pie Face knew what the word "rats" meant. He jumped from Denny's lap and ran around the room, sniffing into all the corners.

"We haven't any rats," said Penny. "I'm sorry, Pie Face."

"Maybe we could get some," Denny said.

"Heavens, no!" said Mother. "Don't you dare bring any rats into the house."

"Never mind, Pie Face," said Penny soothingly, as she picked up the little dog. "*I* like you, anyway. Size isn't everything. Come on, Denny, let's take him out in the yard and show him off."

"I suppose we'll have to," grumbled Denny. "We can't keep him hidden all the time."

The twins carried Pie Face into the yard and set him down. Just then Mr. Kelly-the-Cop came along. He stopped and looked. Then he looked again. "Call that a dog?" he chuckled.

"Of course," said Penny. "He's a member of the Kennel Club, and only dogs belong to that."

"Well," said Mr. Kelly, as he continued on his beat, "I guess he's all right if you like little dogs. Now me— I like a Doberman pinscher. They're big dogs—and fierce—just what a cop needs."

Pie Face paid no attention to Mr. Kelly-the-Cop. He strutted around the yard feeling proud to have a big house and yard to take care of.

All of a sudden he heard a loud "Woof!" A huge brown-and-white creature had jumped the fence and was coming toward him.

"Arp!" said Pie Face fiercely, ready to protect his yard from the strange dog.

But King, the collie, didn't want to fight. The big dog galloped over to Pie Face and crouched down on his elbows, his long, furry tail waving. Pie Face knew that meant "Let's play!"

Round and round the yard they ran. Pie Face thought it was a fine game of tag—until he got caught. One flip of King's heavy paw sent the little terrier sprawling. King waited until Pie Face got to his feet. Then off they raced again.

Pie Face had just dodged between King's front feet when he heard a snort. He stopped so suddenly that King tripped over him, and they both fell in a heap. Pie Face picked himself up and went to investigate.

The snort belonged to a bowlegged bulldog. He was standing with his nose pressed against the fence, and he looked very lonesome.

The bulldog leaped at the fence as if he wanted to come over and join King and Pie Face. But he was too fat and clumsy to jump so high. Then he gave up trying to get *over* the fence and tried to get *under* it. He stuck his nose under the fence and snorted, but his body was much too big to follow his nose. He was so fat that he wheezed with every move he made.

"Hi, Muggsy," called Penny, "you'll have to go on a diet if you want to get through there!"

But Pie Face didn't have any trouble. He squirmed under the fence in a jiffy. Muggsy wheezed forward to give him a friendly sniff. The bulldog's big wrinkled

nose toppled lightweight Pie Face right off his feet. He scrambled up again, looking very much surprised. Muggsy wheezed loudly.

Penny and Denny laughed. "Well," said Denny, "I've heard of being blown over by a *sneeze*, but it only takes a *wheeze* to knock over this little pooch of ours. Come on, King! Let's put that sissy dog in the house and go play!" The twins scampered out of the yard with King at their heels.

After a few days Pie Face got used to being left at home while the twins went away to play. He began to find ways to amuse himself.

He discovered that Muggsy and King weren't his *only* neighbors. People lived in the houses, too.

One day Pie Face was going past a back door when he smelled a wonderful smell. Almost like butterscotch pie—only different. He went up on the porch and poked his nose against the screen door so that he could get closer to the smell. It made him so hungry that he couldn't keep still.

"M-m-m," whined Pie Face. "Arp! Arp!"

A lady came to the door. "You sound hungry, little dog," she said. "But I don't have any bones for you. All I have is gingerbread. You don't like gingerbread, do you?" She opened the screen door and held out the gingerbread. Pie Face gobbled it down so fast he almost choked.

Just then Penny and Denny came along. "Here, Pie Face," called Denny. "Quit bothering the neighbors!"

"Pie Face!" said the lady. "What a name for a dog!"

"Pie is his favorite food," said Penny. "*Butterscotch pie.*"

"Well," said the lady, "you can add gingerbread to the list. He just ate a big piece."

After finding out about backdoor handouts, Pie Face called upon the other neighbors on Cherry Lane. Most of them seemed to have learned that he liked sweets. No one offered him any butterscotch pie, but he was still hoping.

One day he decided to visit the big stone house across the alley. He went up to the back door. "Arp?" he said politely. But no one came to open the door. "Arp?" he said once more, but still nothing happened.

This house certainly didn't smell like butterscotch pie—or even like gingerbread. It had an empty, musty smell. The musty smell seemed to come from the basement. Pie Face decided to go down there and explore.

Pie Face had become quite expert at opening doors —if they weren't too heavy. He pushed the basement door open quite easily with his nose.

He was barely inside when a gray blur scurried across his path. "Rat!" thought Pie Face, and like a flash he was after it. He grabbed the rat by the throat, broke its neck with one quick shake, and tossed it aside.

Pie Face looked at the rat and felt very proud of himself. But he wanted someone else to be proud of him, too.

He picked up the rat by the neck and trotted home. Quietly he nosed open the screen door. Mother was washing dishes. He pattered over and laid the rat at her feet. Then he stood back and wagged his tail happily, as he thought how pleased and surprised she would be.

Mother did not notice him at first. "Arp!" said Pie Face. Mother turned around and—

"Eeee!"

Could that be *Mother* making so much noise and jumping up and down? Maybe she always acted that way when she was surprised.

"Take it away! Take it away! Take it away!" she screamed.

Pie Face dropped his tail between his legs and put back his ears. He picked up the dead rat and slunk out the back door. He didn't need anyone to tell him that he should never bring a rat home again.

The days were getting much colder now. One Saturday morning Pie Face looked out of the window and found the ground covered with snow. King came galloping past the house, plunging through the deep drifts and stopping every so often to roll in the snow. Then he shook the snow out of his long fur and started all over again.

Pie Face could see Muggsy snuffling across his yard. When he snorted into the snow it flew up in the air and came down upon his head. Muggsy really seemed to enjoy the snow shower.

"Come on, Pie Face!" called Denny. "Let's go out in the snow."

Pie Face stood on the porch and shivered while the twins played in the snow with King and Muggsy.

"Come on down in the snow," called Denny from the yard. "Don't be such a sissy, Pie Face!"

Pie Face stepped gingerly down from the porch and into the yard, raising his feet high so that they wouldn't be in the snow any longer than necessary. But in a few minutes he was so cold that he ran back to the porch and howled his most pitiful howl until Denny opened the door and let him in.

"All right. Go back in the house then—sissy!" said Denny. Pie Face hung his head at the tone of Denny's voice. But he just *couldn't* stay outside in the cold.

"Pie Face can't help being a sissy," said Penny. "You shouldn't scold him, Denny."

"Well—maybe," said Denny. "Guess I'd better build him a dog door so he can go in and out of the house whenever he wants to. He could open the screen door last summer, but he can't manage this one."

So Denny sawed a small square out of the bottom of the kitchen door. He sandpapered the edges of the square piece of wood and put it back in the opening, with hinges on one side.

"Why, Denny!" said Penny admiringly. "You've made a swinging door!"

"Sure," boasted Denny. "See how it works?" He pushed Pie Face out through the new dog door. The door swung shut, but in no time at all it swung open again as Pie Face scooted back from the cold outside into the warm house.

"Penny and Denny," called Mother as she came into the kitchen. "Here's a letter from Grandmother with

the registration certificate for Pie Face. This proves that he's registered in the American Kennel Club. And look! It tells when he was born. Why—his birthday's today!"

"Oh!" cried Penny. "May we have a birthday party for Pie Face? May we, Mother?"

"Of course," said Mother. "And I'll bake him a birthday pie."

"Will you bake a butterscotch pie?" asked Penny. "That's his favorite kind, you know."

"Ours, too," added Denny. "I'm sure glad we found out about that birthday."

So Mother made a big butterscotch pie with lots of thick white meringue on top. When it was all finished, she held it down for Pie Face to see. "This is for you, Pie Face," she said. "It's your birthday pie."

Pie Face pricked up his tall ears, wagged his short tail, and trotted after Mother while she went to put the pie on the back-porch table to cool. He didn't know about birthdays or birthday parties, but he sniffed and sniffed of that butterscotch pie!

Denny went to invite King and Tim to the party, while Penny hurried to invite Tommy and Muggsy. Mother went out to the store to get some bones for King and Muggsy. They didn't care very much for pie—even birthday butterscotch pie.

Pie Face and the pie were at home alone. He settled

himself inside the kitchen on the window sill. That was the closest he could get to the pie—unless he went out on the cold porch. The window was closed, but at least he could see the pie.

After a while Pie Face dozed. He dreamed that he was twice as big as King, much fiercer-looking than Muggsy, and that everyone was very proud of him.

Suddenly he awakened with a start. He had heard a noise! It wasn't a very loud noise—just the sound of footsteps.

A strange man was climbing the steps onto the back porch. And the man was going straight for the butterscotch pie!

He picked it up in both hands! That was too much for Pie Face. No strange man was going to lay hands on *his* pie.

He jumped down from the window sill and scooted through the dog door.

Before the man knew what was happening, Pie Face was nipping him in the leg with his needle-sharp teeth. The man kicked at Pie Face, but Pie Face was too fast for him. Pie Face dodged and once more sank his teeth in the man's ankle.

"Ouch!" yelled the man, and dropped the pie. He bent over to grab Pie Face, and Pie Face jumped for his throat. The man's big hands pulled Pie Face away and threw him across the porch. The man started to run down the steps. But Pie Face darted in front of him and tripped him. The man rolled down the steps, clawing at the air.

Pie Face staggered to his feet just as a brown-and-white cyclone hurtled over the fence and landed on the man's chest.

"Arp!" said Pie Face. But his welcome was drowned out by King's fierce growl, as the collie bared his teeth in the man's face. The man did not move again.

As soon as Pie Face saw that King had taken charge, the little terrier made a dash for the fallen pie, and began eating it as fast as he could.

King began to bark and Muggsy tried his hardest to get under the fence.

Around the corner came Penny and Denny and Mr. Kelly-the-Cop. For a moment all three just stood and stared.

Mr. Kelly whipped out his gun and pointed it at the

man. "Get up!" he said. The man eyed the growling collie and did not move.

Denny took hold of the big dog's collar and pulled him away. "It's all right, King," he said, and the man got to his feet.

"Hey!" said Mr. Kelly-the-Cop. "I know *your* face. You're Bill McGuff, wanted for robbing the Third National Bank—aren't you?"

"I ain't talkin'."

"You don't have to. Your face is in every police file in the country. Seems to me there's a reward, too, and part of it will buy this collie the juiciest bone I can find." Mr. Kelly patted the big collie approvingly.

"Wish I had a dog like King," said Denny. "Instead of Pie Face."

"Arp!" said Pie Face, when he heard his name.

"Look!" cried Penny. "He's eating the whole pie!"

"Hope it chokes him!" snarled the bank robber. "Look how he bit me! And what's more, he threw me down the porch steps."

"Huh?" said Denny unbelievingly. "Not Pie Face!"

"Say—he did, all right!" exclaimed Mr. Kelly-the-Cop, as he looked at the robber more closely. "Just look at those toothmarks on his leg, and on his throat. A collie doesn't have sharp little teeth like that. Looks as if Pie Face is the hero!"

"See, Denny," said Penny. "Pie Face isn't a sissy— even if he does look like one! He's the most wonderful dog in the world." She picked up Pie Face and gave him a big hug. Pie Face licked her hand. He felt very happy—and very full.

Mr. Kelly was questioning the bank robber. "How'd you happen to be on the porch here? After all, this doesn't look much like a bank, does it?"

The bank robber hung his head. "It was the pie," he confessed. "I've been hidin' out in the vacant house across the alley. Couldn't go out to get anythin' to eat. When I saw all the folks go away . . . and leave that pie . . . well . . . ."

"Come on," said Mr. Kelly, as he snapped the handcuffs on the robber. "I'll see you get something to eat—in jail."

"What do you think of Pie Face now, Denny?" asked Penny, after the bank robber had been led away.

"Pie Face?" repeated Denny. "That's no name for a brave dog like ours. I'll *show* you what I think of him. You and Pie Face wait in the house until I call you."

Penny and Pie Face waited impatiently. Denny was gone a long time.

When at last Denny called, Penny hurried down to the front gate. Pie Face trotted proudly beside her. He was holding his ears at a very jaunty angle, and carrying his tail very straight.

Denny pointed at the gate. Penny and Pie Face looked.

In the middle of the gate was a sign. Not just a medium-sized sign . . . not even just a big sign . . . but an *enormous* sign:

BEWARE OF BUTCH THE TOUGHEST DOG IN TOWN!

Picnic in the Pantry

The peppermint stick and the candy bar
Sat and dreamed in the big glass jar.
"We'll see the World," they cried one day,
And hand in hand they ran away.

The gumdrops cried, "We'll come along,"
And the peanuts sang a hiking song.
Off they marched past the sugar bowl
And hippity-hopped Mount Jelly Roll.

The day was warm; the day was sunny.
They stopped to rest by the Lake of Honey.
The peppermint stick jumped in to swim
And the candies tumbled after him.

Oh, woe! Oh, grief! A sad mistake,
For who can swim in a sticky lake!

They pulled and tugged but it held them fast
Till Mr. Butter helped at last.
He greased them up and round about,
And at last they were able to slide right out.

Then they all ran back to the candy jar,
And the Peppermint cried, "Let's stay where we are!"

When the children came for a candy treat,
Everything tasted strangely sweet,
And Bobby said, "Say, isn't it funny?
Even the peanuts taste like honey!"

RINGER

Ringer, the monkey,
Liked to swing by his tail.
He'd whistle and sing
And deliver the mail.

There was a letter for Leo,
The lion so-o-o-o-o big;
And a package for Peter,
The fat little pig.

Ringer climbed trees
And flew through their tops.
He'd swing by his tail
Till he looked like a mop.

But the letters he carried,
And the packages, too,
Fell to the ground.
What a *hullabaloo!*

The animals came running——
It looked like a zoo.
Poor Ringer was sorry,
But what could he do?

He picked up the packages;
He sorted the mail,
Then climbed to the treetops
To swing by his tail!

PEPPERMINT

By Dorothy Grider

Once there was a cat named Candy. She was called Candy because she lived in Mr. Dobby's candy store.

One day Candy had four little kittens in her basket behind the stove.

When Mr. Dobby saw the little kittens, he gave each one of them a candy name.

He named the little tan and white striped kitten Caramel.

The black and white one was called Chocolate Drop.

The orange one with the white face was Lollipop.

And there was little Peppermint who was all white and very thin.

Peppermint was unhappy because she did not have beautiful spots and stripes like her brothers and sister.

After school, when the children came to the store to buy candy, they said, "Oh!" and "Ah!" when they saw Lollipop and Chocolate Drop. But when they saw poor little Peppermint, they said, "Oh, my, isn't the little white one frail? Is she sick, Mr. Dobby?"

185

Mr. Dobby liked all of his cats, but he was much too busy to take care of so many pets. Candy was a great help in chasing the mice away, so she would stay at the store. But the kittens would have to find other homes.

Mr. Dobby put a big sign in his window.

Mr. Dobby was a wise man. He knew how much little boys and girls like candy. He knew that if they spent their candy money for a kitten, they would be kind and gentle to it.

Lollipop was the first kitten to go. A little boy brought fifteen pennies held tightly in the corner of his handkerchief. He was very happy to carry Lollipop home.

A little girl in a red coat came next. She couldn't decide between Chocolate Drop and Caramel. Finally she carried the black and white kitten away.

Now only Candy, Caramel, and Peppermint were left.

Late the same afternoon a little boy and girl left their wagon at the door and came into the candy store.

"We'd like a kitten, sir," the little boy said.

In a few minutes Caramel rode away in the wagon with her two new owners.

That left Peppermint all alone with Candy and Mr. Dobby. Days went by, but no one offered to buy the little white kitten, so Mr. Dobby took the sign out of the store window.

It was not many days before Peppermint's fur was a dirty gray because she spent so much of her time in the storeroom hiding behind the boxes and barrels.

One afternoon the children rushed into the candy store. They were excited as they told Mr. Dobby about the Cat Show they were going to have at school. Caramel, Chocolate Drop, and Lollipop were all going to be there.

Peppermint peeked out from behind a big box. She heard the children talking and she wished she could be in the Cat Show, too.

The children ran home to get their kittens ready. But one little girl, in a worn-out sweater, stayed behind. She was rubbing her eyes and looking very sad.

"What's your name, little girl?" Mr. Dobby asked.

"Barbara," the little girl answered between sobs.

"What is the matter?" Mr. Dobby asked. He didn't like to see little boys and girls unhappy.

"I—I don't have a kitten," Barbara sobbed.

"Dear me," said Mr. Dobby.

He had grown very fond of Peppermint, but when he saw how unhappy Barbara was, he said, "You may have Peppermint."

Barbara was too happy to speak. She picked up Peppermint and hugged her close. "Thank you, Mr. Dobby," she said and ran all the way home to her mother.

Barbara's mother had been washing clothes, but she stopped to hear all about the Cat Show and Mr. Dobby and Peppermint.

"We'll have to give Peppermint a bath," Barbara's mother said when she saw the soiled white cat. "She'll never win a prize looking like this."

She took the dirty little kitten and put her in the tub of soapy water.

Peppermint didn't like having a bath. She jumped out of the tub—right into the pan of bluing.

Barbara started to cry. She knew Peppermint was ruined. But her mother caught the kitten, wrapped her in a towel, and put her in the sun to dry.

The next morning Barbara's mother tied a big pink ribbon around Peppermint's neck and put her in a basket so Barbara could carry her to school.

When Barbara reached school all the other boys and girls were proudly holding their kittens. They wondered what Barbara had in her basket.

One by one the children took their kittens up to the front of the room. Finally it was Barbara's turn. Carefully she took Peppermint from the basket and held her up for all the children to see. How surprised they were!

Peppermint was no longer a soiled white kitten. She was a beautiful, fluffy *blue* kitten with a pink bow around her neck.

"Oh!" said some of the children. "A blue kitten!"

"She's beautiful!" said others.

"She must have first prize," someone else said.

So Peppermint did win first prize at the Cat Show. She was the happiest kitten in the schoolroom, and Barbara was the very happiest little girl.

The Lady Who Knew Best

Thomas McGillicuddy was a window-washer in the biggest building in town. He worked like a beaver all day long, from the top to the bottom and back again. He had been doing that very thing for twenty-seven years, and in all that time he had never spilled a drop of water.

Then, one day, when he was up on the very top floor, Thomas bumped *bang-spattle* into his wash pail. Over it went. "Oh, dear," said Thomas, "to think this should happen after twenty-seven years! I feel terrible!"

But there was a lady down below who felt even worse. "Figs and frog-legs!" she exclaimed, stamping her wet foot and shaking her wet fist. "Just wait till I get up there, Mr. Window-washer!"

The lady began to climb up the side of the building, like a fly. "Stop!" shouted the people down below. "You'll fall!" But she was an I-know-best kind of lady so she didn't stop. Not her!

"Now," she said angrily, when she had climbed all the way up to Thomas McGillicuddy, "what do you mean by spilling water on *me*?"

"Sure and I didn't mean anything," Thomas replied in his polite voice. "The pail slipped. I'm sorry, ma'am."

"Oh, you wicked man!" cried the lady, bobbing her wet head and shaking her wet finger. "I'll call a policeman!"

She turned around to look for one, and that was when she saw how high she had climbed. "*Oh, oh!*" she gasped "How did I ever do it?"

Now you know, it is very easy to climb *up* and very hard to climb *down*. Especially if you see hundreds of people below, all shouting "Don't move" and "Hang on" and things like that.

"You'd better sit down," Thomas said very politely. "Would you care for half a sandwich?"

The lady sat on the window ledge, but she was much too frightened and angry to eat. Soon a fire engine came and the firemen spread a net. "Jump!" they called.

"Gracious, *no*, you silly men," said she. *"Never!"*

They put up their highest ladder, and a fireman climbed it to carry the lady down.

"Go away!" she cried. "I wouldn't go down that wobbly ladder for a million dollars!"

Then a policeman called up and told the lady to climb down with her eyes closed. But she wouldn't do that. And a man in a helicopter stopped by and told her to jump in with him. But she wouldn't think of doing *that!*

Pretty soon the sun began to set, and the lady grew very tired. "I'll be up here forever, you wicked man," she cried.

"Well, yes, I guess you will," said Thomas. "Unless you go down the way I do."

"How's that?" the lady demanded.

"First I open the window," said Thomas. "Then I step inside the building and ride down the elevator."

So that was what they did. On the way down in the elevator the lady said very crossly, "I'll bet you thought of this a long time ago."

"Well, yes," said Thomas with a polite little smile. "And the next time someone says, 'I'm sorry, ma'am,' you'd better say, 'Quite all right.'"

Those Cats

By Virginia Cunningham

Miss Simpson looked hopefully out the front window. She moved the red geraniums so that she could look all the way down the street.

What was that . . . ?

Yes, it was! It was Mr. Tooks, the postman. Miss Simpson hurried out the front door and down to the gate.

"Good morning, Mr. Tooks," she called. "Any mail for me today?"

Mr. Tooks shifted the heavy mailbag and leaned against the gatepost. "Well, now, let's see," he said. He wet his thumb against his tongue and began sorting through the letters. "Two for Miss James—one for Doc Brown—and one for Mrs. Hilton from her son up in Coal City—a couple of bills for Hank Peters—and— and that's all for this street. Nothing for you today, Miss Simpson. Sorry."

"Oh," said Miss Simpson, trying not to sound disappointed. "Oh, well, that's all right."

"You expecting something special?" asked Mr. Tooks. "Nothing wrong with your brother's family, I hope?"

"No-o," said Miss Simpson. "Well, that is—I invited my niece to come and live with me, but she decided to take a job in the city instead. I told her to write me if she changed her mind, but I guess she hasn't. It's all right, of course, but—well—I'm lonely! I'm tired of living all alone in this big house."

"Hmm," said Mr. Tooks. He pushed his hat to the back of his head and pulled his left ear, the way he always did when he was trying to think.

"That's too bad," he said after he had thought a bit. "But 'taint hopeless. Tell you what you need—a nice cat!"

"A cat!" said Miss Simpson. "Why, I've never had a cat in my life."

"All the more reason to get one now," said Mr. Tooks. "There's nothing like a cat for company. You can talk to it when you want to, and when you don't want to, you don't have to. It's neat and clean and it will catch mice. Don't know what more you could ask."

"But I—" began Miss Simpson.

"Take my word for it," Mr. Tooks interrupted. "I know all about living alone. And I know cats. Why, my cat Susie is the best friend I've ever had. You should see her run to me when I come home from work. And talk about purring!"

"I'm sure she's very nice," said Miss Simpson politely, "but—"

"Yes, she is nice," Mr. Tooks said quickly. "And so are her kittens. She has two kittens right now—an orange-colored one and a black-and-white one. Which do you think would be prettier?"

"Why," said Miss Simpson, still trying to be polite, "they're probably *both* pretty."

"Good!" exclaimed Mr. Tooks. "That's what I hoped you'd say. Only thing better'n one cat—is *two* cats. I'm right pleased, Miss Simpson, and I know you will be, too. Well, good-by now. See you after lunch."

He was off down the street before Miss Simpson could guess what he meant.

"What is he so pleased about?" she puzzled. "What does he mean?"

But she couldn't stand out by the gate wondering about Mr. Tooks, no matter how puzzled she was. She earned her living by sewing, and she had to get busy.

Miss Simpson worked hard all morning. She worked so hard that she forgot all about Mr. Tooks. At noontime she stopped for lunch.

She was just finishing eating when the doorbell rang. Three long rings and a quick one.

"Why," exclaimed Miss Simpson, "that's Mr. Tooks's ring. Perhaps he found a letter for me after all." And she hurried to the door.

"Hello," said Mr. Tooks. "Here they are."

"Who?" asked Miss Simpson. But she had a queer feeling that she knew the answer.

Mr. Tooks turned sideways so that she could see the big brown leather mailbag on his back.

Over the edge peeked a little furry orange face. Right beside it was a black-and-white face.

"Oh," said Miss Simpson. "Oh, my!"

"Here you are," said Mr. Tooks. He swung the bag off his shoulder, took out the kittens, and handed them to Miss Simpson.

Without knowing just how it happened, Miss Simpson found herself with a wiggly, furry armful.

She took a deep breath.

"But I don't want two cats!" she declared, and tightened her lips so hard that her chin wiggled.

The orange kitten cocked its head on one side. Then it reached up a soft, furry paw and patted her chin.

The black-and-white kitten began to nibble on Miss Simpson's dress buttons.

"Say, now," declared Mr. Tooks, beaming fondly. "Isn't that cute? *They* want *you*, all right. Why don't you just keep them awhile? If you don't like them after a week or so, I'll take them back."

"Well-ll," said Miss Simpson slowly. "Well, I guess that's fair enough. But *one* cat is plenty. I'll try just one cat."

"Two are easier to take care of," said Mr. Tooks persuasively. "They'll keep each other company and they'll keep each other clean, too."

"Just one," said Miss Simpson firmly.

Mr. Tooks shrugged his shoulders, then a sly twinkle came into his eyes. "*Which* one?" he asked.

Miss Simpson thought about the orange kitten's soft paw patting her chin. "The or—" she began.

Just then the black-and-white kitten started to purr. It was the friendliest sound that Miss Simpson had ever heard.

"The black—" she started to say, but Mr. Tooks was talking again at high speed.

"Shame to separate them," he was saying. "They sure will miss each other. Never been apart a day in their lives. Too bad you can't take them both. My, they'll be lonely."

Miss Simpson began to feel as cruel as a wicked witch in a fairy tale.

"Of course," went on Mr. Tooks, "if you can't afford to feed two cats, I wouldn't want you to have them and let them starve."

"Starve!" said Miss Simpson. "Oh, I'd never do that. I can afford to feed them both, but—"

"That's good!" exclaimed Mr. Tooks heartily. "That's fine. I'm glad you decided to take them both. I know you'll be happy—all three of you. Good-by, now."

The next minute he was through the gate and half-way down the street.

"Mr. Tooks, Mr. Tooks," called Miss Simpson, but he didn't seem to hear her.

"Oh, my," said Miss Simpson. She looked down at the kittens. They were both purring like teakettles.

"Well, I declare," she said. "Two cats. What will I do with them?"

Miss Simpson took the kittens into the kitchen and put them on the floor. They stared around at the strange room with curious, frightened eyes, but they were far more curious than they were frightened. In a minute they started to explore their new home. They sniffed at the stove legs, at the table, and at all the other chairs. They crawled under the refrigerator and peered out at Miss Simpson like tigers in a den.

"What shall I name them?" thought Miss Simpson as she fixed a bed for them under the stove. And she began to say over all the cat names she had ever heard of—Smoky, Snowball, Inky. No, those names didn't fit. The black-and-white kitten had too much black fur to be called Snowball and too much white fur to be called Inky. She was white all down the front and up on her shoulders. She looked as if she were wearing an apron, a white pinafore apron.

"Pinafore!" said Miss Simpson. "That's what I'll call you. Pinafore. And Pinnie for short."

Then she looked for the orange kitten. Of course an orange kitten couldn't be named Snowball or Inky. And she wasn't smoky colored, either. She was—why, she was just the color of *orange marmalade!*

"Marmalade," Miss Simpson said aloud. "That's a good name for you."

"Here, Pinnie. Here, Marmalade," she called. At the friendly sound of her voice, the kittens came running. They sniffed at her fingers. Miss Simpson stroked their soft fur and tickled them under their chins. The kittens liked that. They purred and rubbed their heads against Miss Simpson's hand.

Just then a fly came buzzing along. Pinafore dashed after it, but Marmalade started to investigate the wastebasket. She put her paws up on the edge and looked in. Pinafore came over, too. Bang! Over toppled the wastebasket. Clatter, bang, crash!

Pinafore and Marmalade scooted under the stove and looked the other way as if they had never seen the wastebasket. Then they began to wash themselves. When Marmalade had finished washing her own paws, she reached over and began to lick Pinafore's ears. The black-and-white kitten purred happily. She shut her eyes and curled her tail around her feet. Marmalade's eyes shut, too. Soon they were both curled up and sound asleep.

Miss Simpson went back to her sewing. *Whirr-rr* went the motor of her electric sewing machine. "I wonder if the cats will think I am purring, too," thought Miss Simpson.

The blue curtains Miss Simpson was making took a long time. At last one pair was done. She got up and went over to her worktable to get the second pair.

When she turned back, the blue curtain she had just finished was in a heap on the floor.

All of a sudden it puffed up like a balloon. It went whirling around in a circle as if it were alive.

Just then the orange kitten came into the room. She stared at the whirling curtain. She crouched low —then, jump! She landed on it with all four feet at once. *R-r-r-rip!* the blue curtain tore in two. Out of the rip popped Pinafore. She went chasing after Marmalade as fast as she could go. And Miss Simpson went chasing after both of them.

"Those cats!" she thought. "Oh, those naughty cats! I'll give them back to Mr. Tooks tomorrow."

Round and round the room went the kittens. Over chairs, under chairs, around the sewing machine. Bang! Over went the thread cabinet. Green, red, yellow, and purple spools went flying every which way. The kittens tried to chase all the spools at once.

A big red spool rolled right under Miss Simpson's foot. Wham! Down she went.

When she looked around for the kittens, they were huddled under a chair. They looked so scared that Miss Simpson couldn't help feeling sorry for them.

"Here, kitty-kitty," she coaxed. "You couldn't help it. Don't be afraid. Just be glad I didn't fall on you."

But the kittens didn't budge. They shrank back farther under the chair. Miss Simpson couldn't bear to have anything afraid of her—not even naughty cats that she was going to send home tomorrow.

"I know what kitties like," she said. "Some warm milk. Come, kitties."

She went out into the kitchen and fixed the warm milk. She poured some into a white dish. That was for Pinafore. Then she poured some in a yellow dish. That was for Marmalade.

"Here, kitty-kitty," she called again.

The kittens could smell the warm milk. They came out from under the chair and began to drink. But they both drank out of the yellow dish. Lap-lap-lap went their little pink tongues. Lap-lap-lap. When the yellow dish was empty, they both drank out of the white dish. Their tails were stuck up in the air side by side.

When the milk was all gone, Miss Simpson put the kittens out in the back yard to play. "Thank goodness there's a high fence," she thought. "They can't get into mischief and I won't have to worry about their getting away." She watched them for a moment. They were scampering all over the yard, poking into everything with their curious little noses.

By this time Miss Simpson decided that she was ready for her supper, too. When she was through eating, she called the kittens to come and get the meat scraps.

"I'll give you plenty to eat while you're here," she told them. "But tomorrow, back to Mr. Tooks you go."

The kittens didn't understand what she said, but they did understand about the meat scraps, and they purred happily.

Miss Simpson went into the front room and sat down to read the evening paper. The kittens followed her and began sniffing about the room. Soon Marmalade discovered the tassel on the window shade. She batted it with her paw, and the tassel swung back and forth. Marmalade batted it again.

Pinafore jumped up on the window sill, too. She caught the tassel in her teeth and began chewing on it.

"None of that!" cried Miss Simpson. "No, no!" And she put up the window shade so that the tassel was out of reach.

Pinafore watched that swaying tassel. Back and forth it swung, and Pinafore's head went back and forth with it. Gradually the tassel stopped swinging.

Pinafore jumped up on the footstool—and then to the chair—and then to the table—and then onto the window ledge right under the tassel. She took the tassel in her teeth and made ready to jump down again.

Su-wish! went the window shade as Pinafore leaped. *Su-wish!*

Miss Simpson looked up. The black-and-white kitten seemed to be flying straight through the air, with the window shade billowing out behind her. Just then the shade caught on its roller and started to snap back.

"Let go! Let go!" shrieked Miss Simpson.

But Pinafore had already felt the warning jerk. She let go of the tassel and dropped to the floor. She stood there shaking her head as if she wanted to make sure her teeth were still in her mouth.

"Oh, you silly kitty," laughed Miss Simpson as she fixed the window shade.

But the black-and-white kitten did not watch. She turned her back on the window as if she had never seen a curtain tassel—and never wanted to.

Miss Simpson picked up both kittens and took them out to their bed under the stove. "I don't know how *you* feel," she said, "but I've had quite a day."

Then she went to bed herself. She was just dropping off to sleep when something landed plop! on her right foot. And something else landed plop! on her left foot. Then she heard a soft purr-rr-rr.

"Oh," said Miss Simpson aloud. "The cats!"

The kittens came bouncing up to the head of the bed and licked her hand as if to say, "Here you are! We looked all over for you!" Then they trotted back to the foot of the bed and curled up with their heads on Miss Simpson's toes. They made very cozy foot warmers.

"I guess," Miss Simpson murmured as she dropped off to sleep, "I guess I can try to keep them one more day."

The next day was Tuesday. After breakfast the cats

followed Miss Simpson into the sewing room. She gave them some old empty spools to play with so that they would keep out of mischief.

When Mr. Tooks came by she told him that she would keep the cats just one more day.

"I've named them Marmalade and Pinafore," she told him. "I hope you don't mind."

"What?" said Mr. Tooks. "Why didn't you name them Strawberry Jam and Overalls?"

Miss Simpson looked hurt. And then she saw the twinkle in Mr. Tooks's eyes and knew that he was joking.

"Well," he said, "have to be going. Hope the kitties behave themselves."

"Oh, they're playing with some spools," Miss Simpson said. "They're good as can be."

But by afternoon the kittens were tired of the spools. They sat by Miss Simpson's feet and cried. Miss Simpson went right on sewing.

Whirr-rr went the motor. All of a sudden Marmalade jumped up on Miss Simpson's lap. And then onto the machine. The next minute Pinafore was beside her. They cocked their heads on one side and watched the needle busily stitching up and down. Suddenly Pinafore put out a paw to stop the flying needle.

"Oh, oh!" shrieked Miss Simpson. "You'll be hurt." She stopped the machine just in time. "No, no.

Mustn't touch," she scolded, and she spanked Pina-fore's paw and put her down on the floor. "Be a good kitty,"—*like Marmalade,* she started to say. But she didn't. For Marmalade wasn't being a good kitty. She had the thread in her mouth and was unwinding the whole spool.

Miss Simpson spanked more than Marmalade's paw. Then she put both cats out in the kitchen.

"You go back to Mr. Tooks the first thing tomorrow morning," she declared as she shut the door.

"Meow!" came from the other side of the door. "Meow! Meow!"

Miss Simpson went back to work. But after a while she began to think that the cats had been *very* quiet for a *very* long time.

"I wonder what they're up to," she said as she tip-toed to the kitchen door and listened. Not a sound. She opened the door a crack and saw Pinafore asleep under the stove. She opened the door wider. There sat Marmalade in the sink. The orange kitten was holding out her paw to catch the water from the dripping faucet and she was calmly washing her face!

Miss Simpson giggled. At the sound of her voice both cats jumped up and came running to meet her. They rubbed against her legs and purred loudly.

"Why, look at that," said Miss Simpson. "I believe you're glad to see me."

The kittens purred louder. And all afternoon they were as good as kittens can be. They took cat naps in the sunshine, they played with the spools, and they chased their tails. After supper when Miss Simpson sat down to read the evening paper, they came and curled up in her lap as if they belonged there. After a while Miss Simpson went to start the water for her bath. The kittens followed her. As usual they had to investigate every corner of the room.

They put their paws on the rim of the bathtub and stared with fascinated eyes at the splashing water. They jumped up on the rim of the tub and walked around it. Miss Simpson went into the bedroom.

All of a sudden she heard a SPLASH! Splish-splash!

"They've fallen in," thought Miss Simpson, and she

rushed for the bathroom. Just as she reached the door a wet orange streak whizzed past her. A black-and-white streak was right behind it.

The streaks whizzed across the room and hid under the bed. Miss Simpson got down on her knees. Two sets of gleaming eyes stared back at her. The kittens were soaking wet—but not hurt. They were so big-eyed with amazement that Miss Simpson burst out laughing.

"Curiosity killed a cat," she said. "I've often wondered what that old saying meant, and now I know."

In a little while she coaxed the kittens to come out. She rubbed them dry with a soft towel. The kittens began to purr. Marmalade reached up and patted Miss Simpson's chin. Miss Simpson put an old blanket across the foot of her bed and laid the kittens down on it gently.

Somehow on Wednesday morning Miss Simpson just didn't happen to see Mr. Tooks go by. So of course she couldn't give the cats back to him.

On Thursday morning Mr. Tooks came along as she was watering the petunias by the gate.

"Good morning," he called. "How are Applesauce and Apron?"

She was so busy scolding him for saying the wrong names that she forgot to tell him that she thought two cats were too many.

On Friday morning Miss Simpson put the cats out in the yard while she did her weekly cleaning. When she was through she sat down on the porch to rest.

There was a rustling in the bushes beside her and out jumped Marmalade.

"Nice kitty," began Miss Simpson, and then her eyes and mouth opened wide. For Marmalade was carrying a gray mouse up the path very carefully.

"Ee-e-ee," screamed Miss Simpson and leaped up on the porch railing.

Marmalade was so startled that she dropped the mouse and ran up the nearest tree. Pinafore ran after her.

"Ee-ee-ee," screamed Miss Simpson. She was still screaming when Mr. Tooks came by.

Mr. Tooks carried off the dead mouse, helped Miss Simpson down from the railing, and brought her a drink of water.

"There, there, now," he said, patting her hand.

When at last she was calm, they both started looking for the cats. There they were way up on a high branch of the big elm tree.

"Hey, come down," called Mr. Tooks.

"Here, kitty-kitty," called Miss Simpson. Pinafore tried to back down. But her hind legs wouldn't quite reach to the next branch. Marmalade tried to slide down head first. But her legs were too short, too.

"Meow!" they said. "*Meow,* MEOW!" But they did not come down.

Mr. Tooks pushed his hat to the back of his head and pulled his left ear. "Hmm," he said. "Looks bad. But 'taint hopeless. I guess I still know how to climb a tree."

He took the letters and packages out of the mailbag and slung the empty bag over his back. Up the tree he went.

In a few minutes Mr. Tooks and the mailbag with Marmalade and Pinafore in it were safe on the ground. The kittens scampered off as lively as ever, but Mr. Tooks was all out of breath.

"I can't do that very often," he said with a shake of his head. "Tell you what you need—a nice boy."

"A *what?*" said Miss Simpson.

"A boy," said Mr. Tooks. "And I know just where you can get one. My sister is in charge of the Children's Home up at Coal City, you know. I'm going up there tomorrow. Which do you want me to bring you—a boy with blue eyes—or brown?"

"Oh," said Miss Simpson, "I don't—"

"My sister says," Mr. Tooks was going on, "that city kids just love going to a small town like this. She'll be right pleased to hear you want a boy."

"But I—" began Miss Simpson again.

"Oh, just for a week or two," Mr. Tooks went on quickly. "The boy can look after the cats until they're big enough to climb down trees by themselves. The boy will help you, and you can give the boy a real vacation. It's terrible for those poor city kids to be cooped up all summer."

"Yes," said Miss Simpson kindly. "It *is* a pity."

"There," said Mr. Tooks, beaming. "I knew you'd do it. I'll bring back a nice boy Sunday night."

And he was off down the street before Miss Simpson could explain that she didn't want a boy at all. She wasn't even sure she was going to keep the cats.

On Saturday morning Miss Simpson was up bright and early. Since she couldn't stop Mr. Tooks from bringing a boy, she decided to make the best of it. But what would she and a strange boy talk about? "I'll just keep him busy eating," she decided. "Whenever I don't know what to say, I'll offer him something to eat."

She got out eggs and flour and sugar and her best currant jelly and started to make a jelly roll. The cats climbed on a stool and watched every move she made.

"*Meow!*" they said, as if to remind her that it was high time they got something to eat.

"Nothing for you," she told them. "I have a boy to feed." And she put them out into the yard. But she kept looking out so often to make sure that they didn't climb the big elm tree that she almost let the cake burn.

"Maybe a boy *will* help," she thought. "I wonder what color eyes he'll have. I never did tell Mr. Tooks which color I like."

She made some custard to go with the jelly roll and then went upstairs to fix up her brother's old room. She was so busy that Sunday night came almost before she was ready, and there was Mr. Tooks ringing the doorbell. Three long rings and a quick one.

She smoothed back her hair and hurried to open the door.

"Oh," said Miss Simpson. "Oh, my!"

For there beside Mr. Tooks were *two* boys.

"You didn't say which you wanted," said Mr. Tooks. "Blue eyes or brown. So I just brought both. Tim and Bud."

The boys grinned.

Miss Simpson swallowed hard.

"W-W-Welcome home," she stammered. "W-Would you like some jelly roll?"

Tim and Bud slept late the next morning. But Pinafore and Marmalade saw to it that Miss Simpson was up at the regular time. She put the cats out in the yard and got quite a bit of sewing done before she heard the boys coming downstairs.

Miss Simpson scurried to the kitchen and began to get their breakfast. There were big bowls of fresh peaches and cream, pancakes, maple syrup, bacon, and tall glasses of milk.

"Gee," said Tim, the boy with the blue eyes. "It's swell of you to ask us. I've never been in a home like this."

"Neither have I," said Bud, the boy with brown eyes.

They kept eating until Miss Simpson began to think that pancakes would pop out of their ears.

"Whew!" said Tim at last. "I'm full."

"So am I," said Bud. "Where are the kittens? You know, I've always wanted a kitten."

The kittens acted as if they had always wanted boys. They crawled all over them, licking their hands and tugging at their shoe laces. Miss Simpson told the boys how the kittens had climbed the tree and couldn't get down.

"We'll fix that," Bud promised. "I saw something in a movie once that gives me an idea."

"That's fine," said Miss Simpson, and tried to think up something else to say. She couldn't offer them food—not after that breakfast. But Tim had an idea of his own.

"Let's go play in the yard," he said. Bud tucked a kitten under each arm and followed Tim outdoors.

Miss Simpson sighed—and began to bake a chocolate cake. Mr. Tooks was coming for lunch, so she wanted to have something special.

At ten o'clock she looked out to see what the boys and the cats were doing. The cats were walking along the top of the high board fence. Right behind them were Tim and Bud, balancing themselves with arms outstretched like tightrope walkers at a circus.

Miss Simpson shut her eyes and waited for the crash. Nothing happened. She opened her eyes and found the boys—and the cats—safe on firm ground.

"Those boys!" she thought. "They can worry me more than cats any day. Mr. Tooks will have to take them back the first thing tomorrow morning."

She finished icing the cake and went upstairs to make the beds. Suddenly she saw her market basket fly past the kitchen window.

Miss Simpson blinked her eyes and rubbed them.

As she opened her eyes, the market basket flew by again. She could scarcely believe what she saw. Was that really her basket going past the window?

"El-e-vator," came Tim's voice from the ground outside her window. "Elevator. Going down."

Meow! *Meowr!* MEOWRRR!

Miss Simpson rushed to the window. Marmalade and Pinafore and Bud were up in the elm tree. So was her market basket. Bud was putting the kittens into the basket. Tied to the basket was her clothesline, and on the ground below holding the other end of the clothesline was Tim. When Bud gave a signal, Tim pulled the rope and down to the ground came the basket and the kittens.

"See our elevator?" said Bud. "We'll train the cats to climb in by themselves. Then you can let them down out of the tree as easy as pie."

"Want to try it?" Tim offered.

Miss Simpson gulped. "Would you like some jelly roll?" she managed to say.

When she got downstairs, the boys had already helped themselves.

Marmalade and Pinafore were up on the boys' laps begging for their share.

"M-mm," said Bud. "Best jelly roll I ever ate."

"I'll say," Tim—agreed. "Gee, you're the best cook in the world, Miss Simpson. What I mean, THE BEST."

Bud sighed. "Wish I could stay here. We could go fishing, maybe. I bet you could cook fish just right, Miss Simpson."

"Why can't we go fishing today?" asked Tim. "We can dig worms right now. Huh, Miss Simpson?"

Worms! Miss Simpson shuddered.

Just then the doorbell rang. Three long rings and a quick one. Miss Simpson turned and ran. She opened the door and got outside on the porch before Mr. Tooks had a chance to move.

"What's the matter?" he asked.

"The boys," said Miss Simpson. "They want to stay—"

"Fine," said Mr. Tooks. "Wonderful. I told my sister you might—"

"Wait," interrupted Miss Simpson. "It's not wonderful. It's just terrible. They want to go—*fishing*."

"What's terrible about that?" asked Mr. Tooks.

"*Worms!*" shuddered Miss Simpson. "Wiggly, crawly WORMS!"

Mr. Tooks pushed his hat back on his head and pulled his left ear. "Hmm," he said. "That is bad. But 'taint hopeless. Tell you what you need—a husband!"

"What?" gasped Miss Simpson, and turned as pink as the petunias. Then her eyes twinkled. "How many?" she asked. "One—or two?"

"ONE!" said Mr. Tooks. "And I'm the one. How about it?"

Miss Simpson swallowed hard. "C-Come in," she said. "Come in and have some jelly roll!"

the Sleepy Friends of Miss Tabimbo

Miss Tabimbo lived in a tall thin house with thin windows and the tallest, thinnest chimney in town. She had a gate that creaked and a shutter that banged, so she was seldom lonely in a high wind. But on quiet, windless days she thought it would be nice to have a pet.

Miss Tabimbo bought a cat. She was a helter-skelter cat, black and brown and gray and yellow with one black eye and one brown eye and an elegant, long tail. She slept all morning, lying across Miss Tabimbo's feet. It was dreadfully hard to clean the tall thin house, with a helter-skelter cat lying across one's

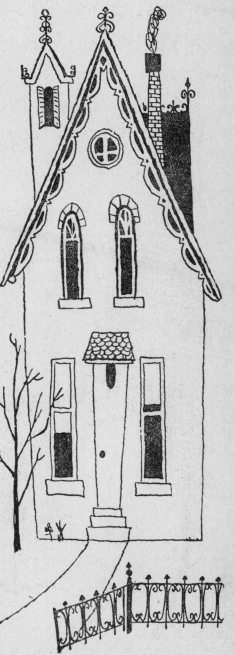

feet, and many times Miss Tabimbo had to sit in her tall thin arm chair all morning so she wouldn't disturb the cat. "Well," she said, trying to be pleased, "at least I'm not alone."

But just the same she bought a dog—a tall thin dog who looked fine in the house. He slept all afternoon curled up in Miss Tabimbo's lap. It was terribly hard to clean the tall thin house with a helter-skelter cat across one's feet in the morning, and a tall thin dog curled up in one's lap in the afternoon. Sometimes Miss Tabimbo sat *all day* waiting for her pets to wake up. "Well," she said, still trying to be pleased, "it's lovely that they sleep so well." She tried not to be lonely on the quiet windless days.

So they lived together, Miss Tabimbo and her morning-sleepy cat and her afternoon-sleepy dog. And because it was so awfully hard to clean the tall thin house with a cat lying across one's feet and a dog curled up in one's lap, the house began to look dusty.

There was dust on the windows and dust on the door knobs and dust on the tall thin chair. After a while there was even dust on Miss Tabimbo, and people passing by began to say, "Whatever is happening to the lady in the tall thin house? I do believe she is turning *gray!*"

She might have gone on getting dustier and dustier, if Thomas Franklyn Binnabut hadn't come to call one quiet, windless afternoon. Thomas Franklyn was seven years old and had a very fine mind. "It's too quiet here," he said as soon as he sat down. And as quick as a witchet he pulled two little gray mice out of his pocket and set them down on the floor.

The helter-skelter cat, who had been dozing in the corner, gave one tremendous leap and began chasing the mice around the room. The noise woke up the tall thin dog on Miss Tabimbo's lap and he jumped down and began chasing the mice, too. Round and round they went, raising clouds of gray dust.

"Katchoo!" said Thomas Franklyn Binnabut. "That's better."

"Katchoo!" agreed Miss Tabimbo. "I really think it is."

All the rest of the day the mice and the cat and the dog ran around the house, upstairs and downstairs, until at last the mice crawled into a little hole in the wall to sleep. While they were running, Miss Tabimbo and Thomas Franklyn had dusted the house.

The next day the cat and the dog never closed their eyes once, because they had to keep watching for the mice. Miss Tabimbo thought it was the nicest arrangement ever. She had plenty of time to do her work, and plenty of company while she did it. In the evening, in the tall thin chair, they all went to sleep together.